MEMOIRS OF AN OXFORD SCHOLAR

CONTAINING

His AMOUR with the beautiful
Miss L———, of Essex;

And interspersed with
SEVERAL ENTERTAINING INCIDENTS

JOHN CLELAND

Dear Sacred Name! rest ever unreveal'd,
Nor pass these Lips in holy Silence seal'd.
Hide it my Heart, within that close Disguise,
Where, mix'd with GOD's, her lov'd Idea lies.
O! write it not, my Hand——The Name appears
Already written——wash it out, my Tears.

POPE

Fredonia Books
Amsterdam, The Netherlands

Memoirs of an Oxford Scholar:
His Amour with the Beautiful Miss L____, of Essex

by
John Cleland

ISBN: 1-4101-0071-5

Copyright © 2002 by Fredonia Books

Fredonia Books
Amsterdam, The Netherlands
http://www.fredoniabooks.com

All rights reserved, including the right to reproduce this book, or portions thereof, in any form.

In order to make original editions of historical works available to scholars at an economical price, this facsimile of the original edition is reproduced from the best available copy and has been digitally enhanced to improve legibility, but the text remains unaltered to retain historical authenticity.

THE EDITOR TO THE READER

After a long intimacy, and much sollicitation, I at last prevailed upon Mr. A——, the husband of Chloe, to write the following sheets. Though the style may be capable of great amendments, I would not take upon me to have an expression altered.

He now retains the greatest veneration for Chloe—He yet idolizes her memory—And, I am credibly informed, she justly deserved it, being, for the sweetness of her temper, and the beauty of her Person, almost matchless.

She died about eighteen years ago. Numbers are now living, who well know the story of the celebrated Miss L——'s running away from her Father-in-Law's. Many were the conjectures—Many the aspersions—malice, envy, and scandal had full scope—While the happy pair, secure in their retreat, and perfectly contented with each other, with contempt heard the insinuating sneer, and the barefaced lie. It was sufficient for them, that two gentlemen of strict honour approved of their passion, and witnessed to their marriage.

I am persuaded, the other characters are truly drawn; and, wishing you may find as much entertainment in the perusal of it as I have done, it is earnestly recommended to you,

By your humble Servant,
The Editor.

CONTENTS

CHAP. I
PREMISES what is necessary to be known 13

CHAP. II
Tells the Cause of the Author's Exclamation .. 16

CHAP. III
Connects well with the former. Some Account of the 'Squire 19

CHAP. IV
Continues the Connection. A Description. A Second Visit to Chloe 26

CHAP. V
The Author thunderstruck—Hurried away to Oxford 32

CHAP. VI
A Letter from Chloe, etc. 35

CHAP. VII
The Author returns to London. His Disappointment 38

CHAP. VIII
A Medley, all of which was not agreeable to the Author 42

CHAP. IX
*The Author writes to Chloe. His Friend Sucessful.
A Letter from Chloe. The Author
goes into the Country* 49

CHAP. X
An Intrigue 15

CHAP. XI
Contains Matters very extraordinary 56

CHAP. XII
*Contains what passed between the
Author and his Friend* 62

CHAP. XIII
*Contains a Letter from Chloe. The Author's
Friend goes to London. His Success;
and other Occurrences* 67

CHAP. XIV
The Author's Second Visit to his Aunt 73

CHAP. XV
*The Author receives a Packet.
Corinna's generous Behavior* 80

CHAP. XVI
*The Author's Friend arrives. They go to
Chloe's Country-House* 86

CHAP. XVII
*Treats of Some Things before the Author
was born, and others afterwards* 92

CHAP. XVIII
*Contains various Matters. Mr. Trueman
is taken ill, etc.* 95

CHAP. XIX
The Author receives an Account of the Death of his Mother. A Strange Revolution in the Family, etc. 102

CHAP. XX
The Author goes to his Aunt's, and to Chloe's. 107

CHAP. XXI
The Author's Friend relates an Account of himself, etc. 114

CHAP. XXII
The Author relieves the Curate, etc. 120

CHAP. XXIII
The Author goes again to Chloe's. Meets with a remarkable Disappointment 125

CHAP. XXIV
The Author goes to London 131

CHAP. XXV
Lucinda's Marriage. The Author returns into the Country 137

CHAP. XXVI
The Author goes to London—To his Aunt's. His Surprise, when he came to his Aunt's ... 146

CHAP. XXVII
The Author goes again to London. Preparations making for Chloe's Wedding. It is broken off. A Duel 155

CHAP. XXVIII
A Letter from the Author's Friend. Chloe's Confinement, etc. 164

*MEMOIRS
OF AN
OXFORD SCHOLAR*

CHAPTER I

Premises what is necessary to be known.

However industrious and ambitious other writers have been to make themselves known, it shall be with equal industry that I will endeavour to conceal myself; and while I entertain you in a plain manner, candid Reader, with a series of real facts, my greatest ambition will be to keep myself unknown.

Birth, parentage and education savour so much of the *Lamp* of an *Ordinary*, that I can by no means consent to follow it. Let it suffice you to know that I was born;—that my parents were of repute; that the escutcheon of my family is inferior to few; and that I was educated in a manner suitable to my birth.

My amusements were boyish, playing at taw, whipping of tops, and all the train of plays, which succeed each other through the various seasons of the year, and employ so many industrious handicrafts in preparing the proper materials for youngsters to squander away their money upon, and to idle away their time in diverting themselves with.

Like other boys, know too, I had my faults— As a great lover of fruit, I frequently robbed orchards, and very frequently my parents' pocket was obliged to make good the damages, there being in those kingdoms, an arbitary property invested in every individual, which empowers him to assert his right to his own, and to so punish the invader, if he is so lucky as to catch him.

This was often the case; and, as there are as many minds as men, you will cease to wonder, that my depredations were not always considered as the tricks of an unlucky boy. Some folk, indeed, have been so very good-natured as to let me go laden with plunder, with an only, *Sirrah! let me catch you here no more*: While others, taking the executive power of the law into their own hands, have severely thrashed me. The third sort, more mercenary in their dispositions, have applied to my parents, and generally charged them with ten times more than the real damage sustained.

I often too played truant—But my master, being more knowing than myself, it was very seldom an excuse would pass upon him. Indeed, if Fame says true, he had been an arch wag himself, and had often put his invention to the rack to prevent that punishment from falling upon himself, which he afterwards so generously bestowed upon others—Thus it happened that a morning's whipping generally followed an afternoon's play—So true it is, that "After pleasure comes pain."

However, these were my chief faults; and, excusing them, I was esteemed a good-natured, generous, high-spirited lad of parts, fond of my books; and, though rare, 'tis true, I was never once punished for any neglect of my exercises.

Here I must beg leave to apologize for, and endeavour, if I can, a little to excuse my playing truant. My master was a great disciplinarian, and so particularly singular in this method from all other of the sons of *Priscian*, that upon no intreaty or public occasion whatever would he consent to give his scholars a play-day. *Wing*'s holidays were the only holidays we had; and, if the almanac-maker had omitted, by chance, one red-lettered day, I am sure all our rhetoric could not have persuaded him to have given us the holiday.

This, I hope, will be admitted as an excuse for my borrowing an afternoon of him now and then, as also for my recommending to the learned Society of Star-Gazers, to be very careful in their annual mystical performances, lest one more should be found of the same temper with my diligent master.

At length, however, I was removed from him to a school of more eminence. Here I began to breathe a little—Here I had no occasion to borrow, where play-days were so generously begged, and as generously given ... Great schools are so well known to the most of those whom I would choose to be my readers, that I shall forbear any account of them —I stayed here 'til my friends thought proper to take me away, in order to send me to an university —In which interval of time!—

CHAPTER II

Tells the Cause of the Author's Exclamation.

I was turned of eighteen years of age when, by my parents' command, I left the public school, at which I acquired some little reputation for my personal courage, and a great deal for the improvement I had made in my studies. I was designed for an university, and Oxford, eldest favourite of the Muses, was the approved one.

As some time is generally spent in preparing things needful for entering, as it seems, into a new state of life, that time I was permitted to pass with Lieutenant-Colonel Standard, a friend of my father's, at his pleasant retirement in a small village, within twenty miles of the metropolis east. Here one evening it chanced, as I rambled about the fields, so deep in thought that I really cannot remember now what it was upon, a young lady about sixteen with her maid, or rather the goddess of the place, with one of her nymphs, passed me; and they had scarcely done so, when a neighbouring 'Squire met them.

It was plain, by his behaviour, he was as utter a stranger to the beautiful creature as myself. He admired her equally; but, while I was endeavouring to number her charms, and was paying a thousand private adorations to every one in my own heart, the brute seized her, and would have ravished a kiss. She struggled, and indeed had the weak assistance of her maid; when, rushing in, I gave him such a blow on his face, as staggered his little understanding, and disabled his less courage from having any opportunity to exert itself. I told him, in a menacing tone of voice, that the lady was under my protection, and the confounded savage tamely kept on his way.

But envy not my happiness, nor envy me the music of her voice, when, in the most agreeable manner, she returned me thanks for my assistance. This was an opportunity not to be lost. I asked, and obtained leave to see her safely home; assuring her, in my company, at the hazard of my life, she should not receive another such affront.

How swift the minutes pass with those we love! —I had already drunk delicious draughts of the sweet poison; and ere, to my thoughts, we had measured one hundred yards, I was obliged, at the end of two miles, respectfully to leave her at her mother's garden gate. She was fearful of asking me in, lest, as she expressed it, her mamma should be angry she had rambled so far from home.

But let me pause a little—The agreeable scene seemed to me to be all an illusion—The gay deceit of a pleasing dream! When, recovering myself, and recollecting whereabouts I was, I found I was within a quarter of a mile of my own residence, where I got just at supper-time, having made a previous resolution to bury all in my own breast. But however I had determined, it was not a virtue of the chambermaid's to be tenacious of a secret. She had whispered it to so many that, before bed-time, the mother was capable of saying every particular by heart: And my behaviour had such an effect upon the generous temper of the well-bred lady, that early in the morning a servant brought me a compliment of thanks, and an invitation to dinner, that she might return them to me in person.

This put me under a necessity of telling the whole affair to Colonel Standard; who, with many encomiums upon Mrs. Worthy, and many more upon the daughter, advised me to go. This I was ready enough to do; and having laid down a plan for my behaviour, I was introduced about half an hour before dinner-time. But what a charming confusion covered the dear creature's face, when I made by appearance! Revive, Apelles; paint it, if you can! ... Such colouring never tinged your Venus!

CHAPTER III

*Connects well with the former.
Some Account of the 'Squire.*

Mrs. Worthy received me with a politeness, equal to the character I had given me of her, and, in a very handsome manner, thanked me for my gallant interposition, in behalf of her daughter: At the same time mildly and prettily insinuating, she had been displeased at her going so far from home, with only a female attendant. We afterwards fell into common discourse, during which I affected all the indifference possible, when I addressed myself at any time to Miss; and, I believe firmly, I was then the youngest and greatest hypocrite in the kingdom: But my eyes were not, I found, under that regulation they ought to have been. This I learned afterwards, and how lucky it was the mother had not observed it.

We were thus amusing our time, when, speaking to her daughter, and calling her by her name, (but, Reader, I will name her Chloe) she said, *My dear Chloe bid them send up dinner.* Just then entered a neighbouring clergyman, and glad at my heart I was, as the conversation would be more enlarged; and, by becoming more general, I imagined I should be the better able to avoid being any way particular to Miss.

We had a plentiful dinner, entirely in the English taste; and, that the clergyman might not be ignorant upon what account I happened to be there, the adventure, with great encomiums upon my behaviour, was minutely repeated. *Oho! then, Sir, you are the gentleman who gave our 'Squire the black eye! He said he got it by a fall. You strike hard, Sir, for it carries the mark of a heavy blow. I cannot say, Sir,* I replied, *that I am any ways sorry for the weight of it. He sought it, and I must have had the meanest spirit to have been present and quietly permitted him, or any other, to use any young person of character with such insolence. But, Sir, if I may be so bold, will you be pleased to inform me who he is?* And the cloth being taken away, and the bottle set on the table, he began ... *With all my heart, Sir,* he answered: *He is master of a considerable estate in this neighbourhood, but is so little resident here that, I dare say, he was an utter stranger to Miss Worthy; or, I believe, he would not have behaved as he did—Though his fortune makes him take great liberties. He has neither father or mother to control him. Unhappily for him, his father died when he was an infant; and, as he was left entirely to his mother's care, her good nature and tenderness for her only child got the better of her prudence: In short, he was so long permitted to do as he pleased, that it was too late, when she perceived her conduct wrong, to make him do as she desired. He took the reins into his own hands, and hurried himself into so many excesses, that his good mother laying it to her heart, died just as he came of age; since which time he lives every where, from horse-race to horse-race, his chief companions being jockeys and cockers, and two or three as rich and as extravagant young fellows as himself: And, I assure you, I intend them no compliment when I say, they are at once the terror and delight of womankind.*

How, Sir, cried Miss, *the delight of my sex!—Stay, Miss, stay ... not so fast ... remember I said "The terror and delight of womankind"—Give me leave, I pray, to explain my own text,* the clergyman replied smiling. *They are the terror of all the innocent modest girls, wherever they come; and the delight only of the loose and abandoned. They are rich, and can pay well. They are the gudgeons the women of pleasure angle for.*

You have here, Sir, his picture at length; all that he is, and, I am afraid, ever will be. In short, though he is now but twenty-three, his constitution seems so much impaired, that the next heir, I imagine, will not be long out of the estate. I expressed my surprize that such a being could exist; but, Reader, you will impute it to my inexperience —I have long since seen five hundred such useless members of society.

When the bottle was finished, the clergyman and the mother set down to backgammon, a game she was mighty fond of and played well at. Miss was bid to show me the house and gardens, and endeavour to entertain me 'till tea time. This commission I observed her to undertake with pleasure, and I flattered myself she was pleased to have an opportunity to be alone with me; at least nothing could have happened more *á propos* for me, nor could the most sanguine lover wish for more than to be alone with the object of his love.

The house was neatly furnished, and the gardens laid out in the elegant modern taste. At the bottom of a long walk was an alcove, which terminated the view, and was commanded by the dining room windows. We sat down here, and I began the conversation by asking, who the gentleman was that dined with us? Miss informed me, he was a distant relation, who had a small living just by, but that he came generally three or four times a week to divert her mamma at the game we left them at: That they were so intent upon it, that she always retired either to read or work; for notwithstanding they were two of the best natured people in the world, they often threw the dice with great earnestness, and though they ventured nothing, they were as desirous of the honour of victory as the greatest gamester could be, whose fortune depended upon a throw.

I then ventured to tell her, I thought the affront

she had the last evening met with the luckiest accident that could have happened, as it had given me an opportunity of seeing, protecting, and becoming acquainted with the loveliest of her sex. I told her, indeed, my passion was young, but yet I was gone an age in love; and that nothing could have induced me to make her such a presumptuous declaration, but an excess of that passion. *I see you, dear Miss, said I, placed so much above me, both as to fortune and merit, that I cannot dare to flatter myself with the least hope of your ever answering my passion—I only ask of you to pardon me, and to pity me. Love, Miss, is a passion not to be controlled by judgment; it it had, mine should have been smothered in its infancy, nor should your ears have been violated with hearing what is at once my unhappiness and pride.*

All this she permitted me to say without offering once to interrupt me, all the time keeping her eyes fixed upon the ground; when perceiving I had done, in some confusion, and with the sweetest voice ever gave words utterance, she answered, *I pardon you, and I pity you—Be not rash;* and, somewhat recovering herself, added, *I have said enough for this time; but, as I am no dissembler, know I am not insensible of your merit, nor do I forbid your addresses: But let me repeat again, be not rash; and I command you to be secret.*

True, indeed, she was no dissembler; for if ever female heart was without guile, it was Chloe's; if ever woman acted without art or design, it was Chloe, dear, charming Chloe! Love regulated all her actions to me, prudence to others.

She had no sooner given me her command to be secret, than she rose, and I getting up likewise (though I could have stayed there forever, so she had been with me) we took a few turns about the garden. As we walked Chloe pointed out to me the various blooms which ranged in formal procession, in the French style, through the lower garden. The roses, *tea roses*, said my fair companion. I turned to gaze upon them, reflecting that their delicate hue was vulgar compared with the tea-with-cream perfection of the skin of her dear face and her ravishing bosom.

The lilies, she said, pointing to the rim of a still, reflecting pool upon which swam two white, imperious swans. The satiny petals of the lilies were the coarsest of stuff beside the dewy perfection of my love's throat and the darling, secret place where her arm was but half protected by the fragile lace that rimmed the sleeve of her simple frock.

As we neared the bottom turn of the lower garden, I looked behind me, toward the house from which we had come, and saw that the privet hedges quite concealed us from the view of those disporting themselves on the broad lawns.

I made bold to encircle my arm about the waist of my fair Chloe. I did so, tentative, afraid that my gesture might serve to raise only her wrath. To my surprized delight, she bent her slender body to conform its slight curves to the length of my own. I lost no time in following up my unexpectedly gained advantage by kissing her fair mouth. She responded to my advance with a hesitant passion of her own.

Still holding the adored one about the waist, I freed one hand, and gently caressed the top curve of her bosom as it swelled shyly from the confinement of the low-cut bodice. I traced my finger over the crescent of the warm flesh that peeked over the lace edging, following the delightful upper curve to the cleft between my Chloe's innocent breasts.

I reached my hand under the trembling creature's left breast and freed it from the stays which enclosed that priceless treasure. Like a poor bird, it shivered fragilely in my hand; but as I soothed it with my stroking fingers, the captured one trembled one last time, then subsided. As I increased the ardour of my caress, the small nipple, its color the color of the most precious topaz, shriveled with an answering passion that reflected the growing ardency in my Chloe's own soul.

She spoke not; her breathing had almost stopped. I knew she had no breath with which to utter even the merest sigh of the most modest reproof.

I kissed her lips again, tasting the nectar-sweetness of her warm breath. I moved my mouth down along the tender pulse spot in her throat. Still caressing the topaz-crowned jewel in my hand, I directed a kiss to its swell.

Breathing in, I almost swooned at the sachet-scent of my love's warm and almost transparent skin. The blue veins around her stiff nipple throbbed with the passion we both experienced. Opening my mouth, I traced the course of the engorged vein with my tongue to its proper destination.

My darling's nipple quivered in my mouth, trembled to the bold onslaughts of my questing tongue. Each pore of that organ opened to the rough texture of the innocent yet aroused nipple. The hard flesh resisted me, made me press my suit ever forward.

My tongue encircled its gem-like hardness and the perfect cone of its shape. The top of my tongue tasted my darling's sweetness; the soft nether part savoured the sharp pointed tip that would one day give suck to our sons.

As I gazed in my darling's eyes, I saw that modesty had overtaken passion and, not wishing to be the cause of distress to my beloved Chloe, I allowed myself but one return to that fount of pleasure. Regretfully did I surrender that perfect orb of flesh to the confines of the stays that molded it and hid from sight its perfection. Having quite composed our countenances, we re-visited the company, whom we found had just got up from play, and were preparing for tea, which was no sooner over than, as handsomely as I could, I took my leave, having first had an invitation to come, and an assurance that I should be welcome, as often as I pleased.

CHAPTER IV

*Continues the Connection. A Description.
A Second Visit to Chloe.*

Home was too near, and my thoughts were too much employed to go directly thither; so I even took another ramble, entirely dedicating my whole mind to my idol. Not that I was without intervening pangs—I was diffident, I knew not of what or whom—Then numberless difficulties threw themselves in my way, as many impossibilities succeeded, and I walked along agitated with the different passions of love and despair; with the greatest reason in the world for the one, and without any one reason in the world for the other—I had every reason to back my love—I had no reason to give for my despair. But love is as ingenious to torment as to flatter: However, love at length entirely prevailed; every other consideration gave way to it, and, in the most pleasing tranquillity of mind happy mortal ever knew, I found myself at home.

Here I had an hundred questions to answer, and a fair opportunity to declaim at large in praise of beauty; but I acted upon the reserve, and answered every question with caution; only praising my genteel entertainment, and contenting myself with barely saying, Miss Worthy was a pretty girl.

At length we retired to our respective chambers, and glad I was to be alone: Then I was sensible how fast my heart was fettered, and every idea rose fraught with the charms of Chloe. This was my first passion, and terrible work it made in my breast... But then I was more happy than thousands; I had disclosed it, and, instead of a repulse, had met with encouragement. No frown had dashed my hopes, nor had an ill-assumed pride denied me pity. I had no meanness to upbraid my passion with—In point of fortune Chloe was greatly above me; her merit was unquestionable, her beauty perfect and matchless, and her figure might have given grace to the famed statue by Phidias. An assemblage of perfections met in Chloe; the sweets of Sabae perfumed her breath, and enchanting eloquence adorned her speech. The smiles of Venus had fixed their residence upon her cheeks, and her swelling bosom was covered with a bloom, more rich than that of the ripe untouched grape.

Such was the person I loved; and, not to have loved her, surely had been stupidity. But then what could I boast? What perfection had I to excite a passion in her breast? Or, if she loved, her passion might justly be deemed mean. She must stoop. A young fellow, not ugly, with some share of understanding, was the utmost compliment I could expect from any unprejudiced person. But *love is blind*—that made all easy again; and the bare possibility that she might love me laid me as fast asleep, as the leaden scepter of Morpheus could have done.

In the morning, when I awoke, I found myself perfectly at ease. My heart in its motion regular, and my mind satisfied with the idea of Chloe, and free from every inquietude which either the difficulty, or the impossibility of succeeding further in my amour, had occasioned.

As I knew it would not be proper, for some days, to visit her again, I made myself happy in my own imagination, continuing my rambles about the woods and fields, with no other companion than amorous Ovid, that great oracle in love affairs, whom I now admitted into the greatest share of my confidence; so heroically resigned did I at once become, upon the full assurance I had in my own mind of her sincerity. However, on the fifth morning, about eleven o'clock, a secret impulse insensibly directed my steps to her abode, when rousing my spirits, and well collecting them together, I ventured to ring at the gate, and ask for her mother. The servant informed me his mistress was gone to pay a morning visit, but Miss was in the garden. *Propitious deities of love*, I thought, *accept my thanks.*

Being showed in, I saw the charming creature reading in the alcove, at the bottom of the walk; and, turning to the servant, I said, *Sir, I see Miss, you need trouble yourself no farther*, upon which he withdrew.

But now my courage failed me, an unusual trembling seized me, and a strange fluttering palpitated my heart: But still continuing to advance, I came within ten yards of her, before she discovered me; when, seemingly surprized, she jumped up, saying *O I bid you welcome*; (and before I could reply) *I have been reading Pope's* Eloise *to* Abelard. *Poor souls! I pity them! were ever two such unfortunate lovers?* I answered, *They were to be pitied—But, Miss, it is the nature of love to mix gall with his honey*: To which she seriously reply'd, *I hope not.*

Here was a fair field open to me, and the chance in view: Nor did I omit making the most of my time, and pleaded my passion with such an artless eloquence, that at last, with a little bashful reluctancy, she gave me leave to love her, assuring me she would deal with me with the strictest sincerity; adding, with the greatest good nature, *I have no notion of giving pain to him I love.*

This was a critical minute; this was an ingenious confession, beyond the utmost of my hopes. Joy flowed in so fast upon my heart, I was scarce able to sustain it; and comfusedly going to thank her, she prevented me, by saying, *My heart approves my choice; I conjure you, be well assured yours does the same.—But I must go dress against my mamma's return—It is one o'clock. Divert yourself here, and I will be with you presently.*

Away she flew, with a thousand blessings after her. Except possession, could there be a youth more happy than myself? I sat down, with my admiration divided between the charms, and the generous behaviour of this agreeable girl; and, while I was in this pleasing reverie, she returned and said, *My mamma has just sent word she cannot be back 'till evening: But, Sir, I hope you will dine with me?*

This was a request not to be denied by me; and, as we were willing to dispense with our officious attendants, we made a quick meal. We were no sooner alone, than we interchanged our vows, and mutually promised to each other fidelity, sealing it with a kiss; which, when I would have repeated, she told me, with some severity, she would allow me no such liberty, 'till a more solemn ceremony had confirmed our contract.

This conduct fixed her, if possible, deeper in my heart. I sincerely begged her pardon, affirming, what was no more than the real truth, that I only attempted a repetition, to convince her of the sincerity of my passion. She believed me, and pardoned me, frankly saying, *The moth that would not be burned must keep away from the flame: And,* assuming a more serious air, *tell me,* says she, *what are your thoughts of a giddy girl, who, at a third interview, has ventured to engage herself to a young gentleman scarce known to her? I expect you to deal with the same sincerity by me, as I have promised to do by you. My dear Chloe,* I answered *excuse me; you ask me a difficult thing. Oblige me first with your reasons, that you have done so? Though I am the happy person, I freely own, it was beyond my most sanguine expectation. Is it so then?* she replied, *and must I defend myself, and to you? I will do it with all the ingenuity I am capable of; and, as you are to be judge, and my defence will be grounded on plain matter of fact, I make no doubt but you will readily acquit me, and accept of such reasons for my conduct as I am capable to give.*

Know then, I had heard, before I saw you, of your good nature and generosity. Other tongues had prepossessed me in your favour; and when I found you to be the same who so resolutely engaged yourself in my behalf, I could scarce believe so much fierceness and good nature could dwell together. But how tender, how amiable was your behaviour afterwards! Love, I perceived, succeeded anger; and, as eloquent as your words were, your eyes looked so many pretty flatteries, love might have borrowed language from them. I was sorry to leave you—I was displeased with my maid for discovering the adventure, lest, through my mother's care, I should have no farther opportunity of seeing you. But how pleased I was when she took the resolution to send you her thanks, and invite you to dinner, my own heart only knows! Thence sprung my confusion at seeing you; and, it was easy to perceive, you played but an indifferent hypocrite, whenever you looked at me. I was fearful of my mother's experience. Had she suspected one look, you would have seen me no more; and lucky it was for us both my cousin came to dinner. Pleased with my conquest, I resolved to act without reserve to you. If you declared your love, I was determined to accept it. Hence the ready compliance; hence your victory over Chloe. I fear I have scarce preserved the decorum so necessary to my sex; but I knew you were soon to leave this place, and I could not bear to let you go and believe you were indifferent to me: That was, at once, to lose you. I had no medium, and I could not consent to give you pain, and at the same time make myself unhappy. Preserve your love for me, and I will endeavour to deserve it; and, believe me, nothing shall alienate my heart from you. We have vowed fidelity; let us be faithful.

It is not easy to imagine with what pleasure I heard a defense so elegantly made; nor did the flattery so artfully played upon me contribute a little to it. I was obliged to confess my own imagination could have suggested nothing adequate; and indeed I should have been at a loss to vindicate a conduct, which, however agreeable to my passion, seemed to stand in need of a vindication to the world. But then, what had the world to do with the conduct of individuals, when society was in no way injured? If it had, we were out of the world's eye; we were the keepers of our own secret, for fortune had hitherto been so propitious, we had neither of us occasion for a confidante.—But I thought my visit had been long enough; and, without waiting tea, I had her permission to retire, with her approbation for so doing.

CHAPTER V

*The Author thunderstruck—
Hurried away to Oxford.*

I went musing along slowly towards home, as happy as desire could wish. Charmed with her ingenious defense, more charmed with her chaste delicacy. My love was sincere and pure: My heart approved her refusal of the kiss, and does to this hour; for, since I fell from the state of innocency I was then in, I have had reasons sufficient to prove what I now assert, *That most of the unhappy young women this town abounds with, have been accessory to their own ruin.* But judge my surprize, when entering into the yard, I was accosted by my father's servant, with a letter commanding my immediate presence in town; for everything was ready, and he designed to go with me the next morning to Oxford.

However disagreeable these commands were, they were such as must be obeyed. I was soon ready, and after the customary compliments at parting, I set out, with a heavy heart, for London. Those only who have parted from what they have esteemed most dear, the childless parent, the weeping widow, or some unhappy youth in similar circumstances, can judge of the situation I was in—Without the least previous notice hurried from all I loved—Not one day, not an hour, not even a minute given to say, farewell.

I knew it must happen, but I did not expect it so soon. I had flattered myself with at least two or three days: In short, I was so totally unprepared to receive the blow, that I trotted on regardless of every place and thing. Chloe took up all my thoughts—I had no room to entertain any other object—What could she think? She would hardly imagine I was under the necessity, under a peremptory order to depart instantaneously. *Civility* (surely will she say) *might have taken leave: If nothing was due to love, something was due to good manners. I was too cheap a conquest, and he rewards me accordingly.* Thus I reasoned in the person of Chloe; but that dear creature, I understood afterwards, was not capable of a suspicious thought.

Under these distracting agitations of mind I arrived at home; and found it too true, that the next morning, at four o'clock, we were to set out. Nothing more than common happened upon the road, and about seven in the evening we drove into the Bear Inn, where we lay, as the landlord was master of the coach.

The next morning, after we had breakfasted, we waited upon the Head of the College of which I was designed to be a member; who recommending a tutor, I was immediately in a borrowed gown and cap matriculated, after which ceremony we returned to his chamber to dinner.

My allowance was fixed at eighty pounds *per annum*, under the management of my tutor, so that I found what money I was to have, was to come through his hands. This did not please me, but I had no remedy. My father stayed 'till everything wanting was put into my chamber, and then left me to meditate on Chloe, who, in all this hurry, was not absent from my thoughts.

In this time I had made no acquaintance in our own college; but, recollecting I had an intimate school fellow at another, I set out the very morning my father returned to London to inquire him out, and was so fortunate as to find him. We renewed our friendship, and were as much together as the times of our college exercises would permit, though it was not long before I had contracted a great intimacy with three or four young gentlemen of my own society. Everything at Oxford contributes to strike a young student with a venerable awe for that sacred seat of learning: But I am not about a description of that place, so shall only say, I retain the most dutiful regard for my *Alma-Mater*, and return to myself.

As I was of a gay and lively disposition, my companions were of the same cast, and I was soon initiated into the social pleasures of the bottle; and, not caring at every turn to go to my tutor for money, I was very early showed into the method of running in debt, which I did pretty considerably, scarce giving myself time to think, when I was to pay for what the impetuosity of my temper hurried me to order. As my tutor kept a correspondence with my father, I received no letters, and I had been here about six months before one was brought me. I looked at it with some surprize, as I was a stranger to the hand; but imagine, if you can, my transports, when I found it came from Chloe!

CHAPTER VI

A Letter from Chloe, etc.

"*SIR,*

If I hold the same place in your esteem, I flatter myself I once did, this will be an agreeable interruption to your studies. When you parted from me, I did not expect to see you again in less than four or five days, as you had observed too frequent visits might occasion suspicion; but judge of my uneasiness, when ten days passed and no sight of you! I did not doubt your fidelity, but was fearful of your health; my love is subject to fear, but a stranger to suspicion: However, my mamma relieved me from my anxiety by saying, *I wonder young Mr. A—has not called upon us again—Maybe he is ill—Let John go this afternoon and inquire.*

I flew to deliver John his orders, and he returned with the following account—That your father had sent for you in a hurry, and that you were at Oxford, but at what College was unknown. This quieted my fears for your health, but could by no means satisfy my impatience to write to you: However, I was obliged to be content 'till we came to London for the winter, when I hoped, by some means or other, to find out the particular College.

It yesterday fortunately happened as I was with Miss M—, her brother, who is of Merton College, came in. I began to inquire into the method of living at the university, and he gave me a pretty general account of their way of life in his own society, adding, *I believe, Miss Worthy, this may serve for the whole, though I seldom am in other Colleges, except sometimes at *****, to see an old school fellow.* His sister immediately asked, *Who is it,*

35

Brother? have I seen him? He answered, *No, it is young Mr. A—; he never was here.*

Lucky discovery! I hastened home, and caught the first opportunity of putting pen to paper, to assure you I am unalterable in my resolution. I continue the same Chloe—Do you? will you continue the same A—? Indeed I do not doubt you. I will trust nobody with this, but put it into the Post Office myself, as I go to the Park.

Oh! I will make you easy in one particular you expressed some fear about. I assure you, my mamma thinks twenty-five time enough to be married so she will not be pressing with me, on that head, especially as she is to part with my fortune on the day of my marriage, if it is with her consent. Now I have written to you, I see no possibility of receiving an answer. I can trust no one to receive your letters; but we shall be in town 'till the middle of April, and you may be sure of a welcome from my mamma, if you come to town. We are in —— Square.

Chloe."

Kind girl! assure yourself I cannot change; I am, and only can be yours. This letter gave me such spirits, that I invited the chosen few to my room, where, being a little too busy with bumpers, we happened to disturb the society, for which the next morning Mr. Trueman and myself were confined to the library for a month, with a swinging imposition of old Tully's to divert us.

This put an end, at least for that space of time, to every scheme for conveying an answer to my letter. The month elapsed, and we were again at liberty. I began to think upon forming some scheme, and many occurred, but all were deficient. I then resolved to go to London myself, and waited upon my tutor for his leave; but he gravely asked me, if I had a letter from my father. I told him, *No.*

Then, Sir, says he, *I cannot give you leave; for I have particular instructions from your father not to let you lie a night out of College without his orders.*

This was a cutting stroke; however, I was not debarred from taking an airing at times, but I was obliged to return by nine. In one of these little excursions along with a gentleman of great vivacity, as I galloped after him, he met a wagoner whistling along by the side of a good team of six horses, and took it into his gallant head to insist upon the way. Instead of complying, the fellow saluted him with a smart cut across his shoulders. My friend rode off, contented with his share; but I, not considering the inequality of our whips, rode up to him, and met with two or three of the same smart salutes; and, to aggravate the insult, he continued whistling. A retreat was judged proper; but the fellow, to jeer us, continued smacking his whip, which occasioned his horses to exert their spirit. Three of them broke their traces; and finding themselves at liberty, galloped across the fields to the driver's vexation, and our no small satisfaction.

Nine months were passed, April drew on, and no resolution taken, no scheme formed; when fortune on a sudden, and when least expected, changed her mind, and threw once more her smiles of favour upon me. In the midst of my despondency, one afternoon a bed-maker came to me, and told me my tutor wanted to speak with me.

CHAPTER VII

*The Author returns to London.
His Disappointment.*

At this time some of my duns, as creditors are named at Oxford, had asked me oftener for money than I chose to hear. Just before the bed-maker came to me, one of these civil importunate gentlemen had been with me: And, as I could not answer his demand, he went from me muttering something about tutor, and I readily concluded I should find them together, but I happened for once to be mistaken. My tutor, when I came, informed me, he had just received a letter from my father, with his leave for me to go to London; that he would acquaint the Head of the College, and there was a guinea for me to take a place in the coach for what day I would. Away go I to the inn, and take a place for the next day but one, sending away to my laundress to be sure to let me have my linen by five o'clock the next afternoon.

When I had packed all up, I waited on my tutor just before supper to take my leave of him, and he very civilly, for the first time, asked me to spend the evening with him. Just at parting he gave me two guineas, saying, he would examine the buttery-book, and if he found he had any money left in his hands, he would account with me for it at my return.

I was two days upon the road, and heartily glad to see my father's house. He received me very tenderly, and told me he had sent for me at the request of a great-aunt of mine, and cautioned me to behave very circumspectly, for she was worth money, and he knew no relations she had so near as our family. Accordingly I went upstairs, and paid my duty to my mother and aunt with the best grace I was master of. London had put new life into me, for Chloe was there! But I found I had only changed one prison for another, for what between my mother and my aunt, it was the fourth day, an age to me, before I had an opportunity of going to wait upon her.

No sooner at liberty than, with the utmost expedition, I hastened to——Square; and when I found the house, to my astonishment, the windows were all closed: However I knocked at the door, and asked for Mrs. Worthy; but was answered, *Sir, my mistress and miss went to Bath yesterday morning.*

Forgive me, Reader, if I cursed my stars, and accused fortune of deceit and willful partiality. What had I to do at London! Chloe was at Bath!—While I was thus biting my lips, and railing to myself, a thought started into my head, that, perhaps she might have written to me to Oxford; and, as I had settled a correspondence with one of my intimates, and had directed him to address to me at —— Coffee House, it was not improbable, if I went there, but I might find a letter from her: And so it happened, for, upon inquiry, the barkeeper presented me a double letter, which I opened with fear and trembling—I was afraid to be satisfied of what I wanted to know—O timorous love!—I read the enclosed one first, which was as follows:

"*SIR,*

I am not so much disappointed at my not receiving a letter from you, as I am at not seeing you. I impute the first to your prudent circumspection, and the hazard of conveying it to me; but I know not what to think of the last. Sure one hour might have been spared from the Muses! No excuse to get to town! I cannot help saying this.—I think proper to acquaint you we set out for Bath tomorrow, my mamma being advised to use the waters—I am very well—but wish to see you—You shall know when we return.

Chloe."

I omit the other, as being foreign to my tale. Just as I had finished reading my letters, who should enter the coffee room but my fellow collegian and fellow prisoner in the library, Mr. Trueman, with whom, during our confinement, I had contracted a strict friendship; and, indeed, I found him on this, and many other occasions, truly deserving the name of friend. We both rejoiced at this chance meeting, for though I knew where to find him, I had not yet had time; and, when he left Oxford, which was a month before me, I had not the least expectation of seeing him in London.

Nothing would serve him, but I must spend the evening with him, which I could not do, as being confined very strictly; so we agreed that he should come and dine with us the next day, and, if a favourable opportunity offered, to get leave for me to sup with him.

He came to the agreement, and my father seemed pleased with my acquaintance; and matters were so well managed, that I obtained leave to go with him and stay 'till next day, upon condition he came with me again to dinner, as he said he was obliged to go out of town in three days. *Come,* said he, as we were going along, *I will show you something of the town. But pray, my friend,* I replied, *where are you going to, when you go out of town? Why, into Devonshire,* answered he, *to a relation's about some family deeds, and I propose to take Bath in my way.*

It immediately occurred to my mind that I must, by some means or other, send a letter to Chloe. Somebody I must trust, and who so fit, as a gentleman who professed himself my friend. I was beginning to unfold myself to him, but he interrupted me, saying, *Pleasure tonight, business tomorrow.*

CHAPTER VIII

*A Medley, all of which
was not agreeable to the Author.*

The first place we proceeded to was the playhouse in Covent Garden, to see inimitable Falstaff, in *The Merry Wives of Windsor*, performed by Mr. Quin. I was indeed entertained, and Mr. Trueman met here with a town acquaintance of as gay a disposition as himself, who, at the first word, agreed to be of the party for the night. Neither of these were kept under any restraint. The doors were locked, if they were not at home by such an hour, and that was all; and, as to myself, I likewise was freed from mine, by permission.

When the play was done, we adjourned to a tavern in the neighbourhood, ordered a supper, and as we wanted no money, called for a bowl of arrack punch. We had no reason to complain of our attendance—*Coming, coming, Sir*, was often repeated. Thus, as happy as young fellows could be, we were diverting the flying hours, when the sudden clash of glass in an adjoining room disturbed us. Up ran the master of the house, with two or three waiters at his heels, to see what was the matter; and, though we had absolutely no business there, as it was no concern of ours, we made part of the company, so much curiosity got the better of good manners.

Passion soon informed us of the occasion of the disaster, which was greater than we imagined; for besides a large pier glass, there was a small curious china dish, lately full (at no little cost) of green peas, both of which were shivered to pieces. This dish had been the messenger of wrong-vented anger, if any is ever vented right. The whole affair was this—A gentleman of no small reputation had appointed his mistress to meet him, and accordingly had ordered an elegant supper for her. She seemed about thirty-two; but, either by way of blind, or some other motive, she brought with her a handsome girl about nineteen. Whether the gentleman was more particular to the young one than he ought to have been, out of more complaisance, or a real love of change, I cannot take upon me to ascertain: But something was, or at least seemed to be done, which roused the devil jealousy; and as upon these occasions decorum is seldom preserved, the first thing which came to hand was made a sacrifice. The china dish, full of peas, was put in motion; but missing the head aimed at, abated little of its force, 'till the glass was shivered at the rude salute.

Both perished, and the landlord vehemently insisted upon being paid for both. The gentleman made no hesitation to satisfy the damage, but gave him a twenty-five pounds bank note; who, after paying himself, laid the remaining change upon the table, when the mercenary disposition of the creature of pleasure appeared in its full light: Not contented with the expense her insolent passion had already occasioned, she was pilfering from the change, and artfully conveying it into her pocket. My friend observing her, thought himself obliged to detect her; but instead of thanks, was answered with, *Dammee, Sir, what is it to you? She is welcome to all of it, if she pleases.*

This behaviour would have brought on a quarrel, but I considered we had intruded into the room and prevailed upon my company to withdraw: Observing to my friend, that his honour was no way concerned, and I could not permit him to engage himself in a duel, contrary to his own opinion; for I had heard him often say, *No w—e in the world was ever worth fighting for.*

This *fracas* being over, we circulated the glass 'till near one, when an adjournment to the celebrated Tom King's was proposed, and with very little hesitation agreed to. In a few minutes we were in the throng of bullies, sharpers, pimps, pickpockets and gentlemen. I shall waive a description of these nightly orgies, lest any should imagine I esteemed them deserving of one.

While we were diverting ourselves with the different, and odd characters of the place, a young gentleman came in, accompanied by two young gentlewomen. It was visible, at first sight, the women were of a different sort from those, who made their nightly appearances here. As the place was pretty full, it was with some difficulty they got seats; but no sooner were they seated, than the game began. Much ribaldry was thrown out, and many low jests passed: At last a fellow, bolder than the rest, offered to kiss one of them. This the gentleman resented—the women shrieked—the house divided. All, who had any sense of honour, engaged in the defence of the strangers, and were opposed by those who had long lost all sense of shame—The juster cause prevailed, and the bully and his adherents were turned out of the room.

The gentleman returned us thanks in a very handsome manner for our ready assistance, assuring us he had never been there before, but having heard much of Tom King's, and passing by from a relation's, where he had supped with his sister and the other young lady, he had inadvertently proposed, and they had as inadvertently agreed, to come in, and see the humour of the place.

Chairs being fetched, they left us, I believe, sufficiently frightened to resolve never to gratify their curiosity again in so imprudent a manner. The company growing thin, Mr. Trueman's acquaintance proposed our going to a bagnio. I hesitated some time at that; but, being too easily persuaded, I consented—So regular, and with so little thought, young people proceed from one scene of vice to another.

As I had agreed to come here, I easily persuaded myself to give into the custom of the house. The ladies appeared, and each singled out his Sultana. Thus, in a moment, forgetful of my honour, my vows, and Chloe, I permitted my love to subside, and caught the first opportunity to gratify my lust!

The girl who fell to my share either had not entirely thrown off all, or else prudently affected some sense of modesty. Leaving the liquorish band to their rowdy devices, Jenny (for that was her name) and I stole to a small chamber furnished with a large bed and the French cabinet named an *armoire*.

Jenny began to draw her pins and as she had no stays to unloose was swiftly naked of all but her shift. For my part, my breeches were as swiftly off, my shirt collar unfastened, when Jenny, reclining among the pillows let out a gasp. I followed the direction of her eyes with my own and saw that my rod, long absent from the pleasures of the flesh, had swollen to fearful size. It sprang from the thicket hairs that nestled at its root; its head was too much for the breadth of one hand; Jenny had need to encircle the demon with both hands extended to their fullest reach.

As I stepped toward the pleasure pallet, Jenny spread her fulsome thighs to their utmost. I discovered there with my bold eye the erect mark of her sex, the crimson centered cleft of flesh whose lips, blushing ever more redly, led inward to the waiting pleasure channel.

My passion, long pent, could wait not a moment more. I lay down beside the wench kissing her moistly, making free with my hands, playing over her plump breasts with their hardened nipples, licking them furiously, arousing her to ever higher fevers of excitation. Wasting no more time in the niceties of the preliminaries I thrust my throbbing member roughly into the delicate channel.

So large had my engine distended that she gasped again at the ferocity of my thrust. But I gave the girl no surcease from the vigorous onslaughts effected by my fearsome member. I reached my hands beneath her waist, raised her luscious bottom with both my hands thus positioning her more advantageously for the thrusts of my rod. I reached down within the sweet cleft and felt with my hands the strength of my shaft as it coupled with her wide-spread nether-lips. Our hairs mingled; our most sensitive parts were entirely conjoined.

Oh! what adorable bliss! what heavenly rapture! what sweetness sublime!

So long had I been without the soothment of her sex that the honey liquid burst from my vessel in a tidal wave of boiling fury. It washed down her thighs and its colour was tinged pinkish with the blood my huge machine had torn from the poor girl's miniature entrance.

I lay back, for the moment, drained of all strength. But the minx's fires burned high still. Her little tongue slipped its humid way through the tufts of hair round my own nipples. It followed its growth down toward my birth knot and ever down toward my listless member.

But rogue that he was!

In no time he stood up again. As firm, as strong, and as large and monstrous as if he had never been tall before. Jenny held him by the shaft with both her firm hands and circled the vermilion head of that impish demon with her pointed, slightly rough tongue. I had to clench my jaw to stop from spraying her again with the sweet juices of passion.

At length she left off her lubricious tonguing of my private part and stretched herself out along me on the bed. This time, resolved not to be so hot in my quest, leisurely I tongued her mouth, exploring the warm, dark wetness of it with growing languor and heat.

I moved next to her ripe, full breasts, first licking at the erect, long nipples, then biting them ever and ever more fiercely so that the poor girl cried out despite her pleasure. I sucked their sweetness, leaving bruises around the nipples where the pressure of my mouth had drawn blood to the surface.

My attention next was placed on that very summit of all pleasure. I spread her knees with my hands, kissing her inner thighs so that the creature squealed time and time again with delight. I next mouthed the golden soft curls that sheltered the central joys of her sex. My spittle wetted and matted that fine moss and I soon found my tongue wandering round the outer portion of that pink shell. The resistant texture of the hair, that smooth resilience of the pearly flesh—such were delights to offer kings. I circled smaller and smaller with my searching tongue till it probed that very center of sensual enjoyment.

Her secret orifice opened to the probing of my ardent tongue. Her rounded bottom began to move in rhythm with the explorations of my own. Sensing that it was time to leave off this occupation, pleasurable though it was, I retraced my steps, kissing again the delicate outer lips, the still-wet moss, the bluish-white skin of her inner thighs, and concentrated myself on the main enjoyments.

Inch by inch, I impaled her with my sturdy rod, now grown to even greater dimension by the preceeding excitations. This time, her pleasure mount fully receptive to the aggressions of my member, she did not gasp with pain; she moaned with pleasure. I thrust; She answers. I stroke; She heaves.

Our rhythms joined. Our passions grew. I push so deep into her that I think I must rend the wench in twain; but her sole response is yet another moan, this, low in the throat.

Our breathing deepens to a growl, then, in unison, to a roar. The bed shudders with the weight and fury of our entwined violence.

Then with a shriek she adds her juices to my own and I discharge with an enormity of passion, my juices boiling over, searing her very deepest vitals.

When we recover ourselves, I asked if I might again call upon her.

Oh, indeed Sir, she replied.

She promised then to show me the Italian delight of which I had so oft heard but which, in truth, I had not ever experienced. This promise, and this behavior contributed not a little to my often visiting her afterwards, at her own lodgings: However let me do myself the justice to own, that when I waked in the morning, with my reason cleared somewhat from the evening's debauch, I grew very uneasy—Chloe filled all my thoughts—Chloe upbraided me—My heart approved her delicacy, and yet I was in the arms of a wanton.

But these generous sentiments soon left me, and I satisfied myself with making a resolution to be true to Chloe, when I had possession of Chloe.— But to my story—When we had discharged our bill, we took leave, my friend and I going into the Park, and his acquaintance about some business. Here I unfolded to him, as much as was proper for him to know, of the affair between myself and Chloe, and entreated his assistance to convey a letter to her, which he readily promised. Easy in this matter, and a full assurance of his friendship, we proceeded home to dinner, and were received, without any suspicion of what we had been doing, with great civility to my friend and tenderness to myself; and I had likewise the pleasure to hear, I was not to be so much confined at Oxford as I had been, my father saying, his intentions were that I should only reside there during the terms.

CHAPTER IX

*The Author writes to Chloe. His Friend
successful. A Letter from Chloe.
The Author goes into the Country.*

Sometime after dinner my friend withdrew with me to my chamber, and while he amused himself with a book, I caught the golden opportunity to write, as follows, to Chloe.

"*My Dear Chloe,*

"This, I am sure, will be welcome to you; and I make no doubt of its coming safe to your hand, it being intrusted to the care of a gentleman in whose fidelity I have the greatest confidence. I called at your house the day after you left London; but judge my vexation, to learn you were on the road to Bath.

"Nothing could have alleviated my grief, but a letter from you, which I was so fortunate to receive. Accept my sincere thanks for that, as well as a former one addressed to me at Oxford.

"Courage, my dear girl, we shall meet and be happy. Assure yourself I am the same, and as free from all suspicion as yourself. Happiness dawns upon me. I have just heard I am not to be under the restraint I have been, and it shall be my fault if I do not make use of my liberty to see you, as often as you will permit. Whatever impatience may attend my love, I will submit it to your direction. I am assured of your sincerity, and assure yourself of mine. You may trust your answer to my friend's care.

*My Life, My Soul!
Adieu*"

This being sealed and delivered to Mr. Trueman, he renewed his promise of conveying it safe; and being at ease now in every particular, we returned to our family. I confess, at this time, I saw my friend leave me with pleasure, as it was only his absence could enable him to do me the greatest service in the world, and which I knew of no other in it so capable of doing.

Some days passed on, in which time I learned I was to accompany my aunt to her dwelling; and, after passing a month with her, return to the university. My father readily came into the request of my aunt's, as he perceived she had a particular liking for me, and he founded great expectations on my being her heir.

In this period of time I visited my Sultana at her lodgings, and continued often to do so, being pleased with an easy access, without the great expense of attending the meeting of her at another place; and without once considering I was accustoming myself to a vicious habit, and allowing my passion to govern me, I imputed my frequent visits to the delight I took in her conversation, and the generous disinterested turn of mind she seemed to possess, and which I esteemed as the first among her many alluring accomplishments: nor did I omit to give a due attendance to the coffee room, impatiently expecting what at length came, a letter from my friend, or Chloe, or both. The first was as follows:

Bath,—

"*My good Friend,*

I was some days before I could get an opportunity to execute my commission, and indeed grew fearful I must leave the place without finding one; but either your good fortune or mine favoured me with one, at last, in the pump room. Entirely unobserved by anyone, I delivered your letter to Miss Worthy, only saying, *Madam, from Mr. A—. I will be here punctually again tomorrow.* I approve your judgment in your choice, and am

> *Yours sincerely,*
>
> *John Trueman."*

The second, from my angel, runs thus:

"SIR,

Bath,—

For some days I have been under great perplexity, at the officious assiduity with which a young gentleman has followed me, but I am now all joy and spirits. I observed constantly something in his hand like a folded paper, and imagining he had taken a liking to me, and wanted to give me a billet, I made a resolution to give him no opportunity. However, as no person is long a stranger here, I soon found he was a young Oxonian. My heart fluttered, and as I have long expected a letter from you by some means or other, my good genius prompted me to alter my mind; and accordingly, the next time I was at the pump room, I observed him close to me, when purposely I dropped my handkerchief. He readily took it up, and, in a very genteel manner, presented it to me, speaking very low, *From Mr. A—;* adding something more, but I only understood, *Again tomorrow.*

"I was impatient to be at home. How happy have a few words made me! I thank you—I rejoice at your liberty—I shall be glad to see you. My mamma is much mended, and proposes soon to leave this place. Thus far I have written, without one thought how you will have it; but I must hasten to a conclusion, and leave that to fortune. You will be sure to know from your friend I have had yours, and, if this must be delayed, that will be some satisfaction to you.

I am yours.

And will be only yours,

Chloe."

This affected me so much, that I was ashamed of my infidelity to this charming girl, and determined to see my Sultana no more. I resolved to be true to Chloe—One part of my resolution I kept, through the departure of my aunt for her habitation, and my being obliged to accompany her, and the other part I might have kept, had I remembered in time, *The moth that will not be burned must avoid the flame.*

We came after an agreeable journey, to my aunt's, north of London about forty miles. This was a neat little house, and I found everything was conducted with great economy and regularity. There were three servants, two of the female kind, and the other a male; a second scrub, who acted in various capacities, as occasion required.

CHAPTER X

An Intrigue.

As my aunt, or more properly my great-aunt, was considerably advanced in years, she lay in bed long, was seldom abroad, and went to bed more early than is even customary in the country—But then a large company frequented the house—Mercenary, talking gossips, who brought all the news of ten miles round to divert the old woman, at her neighbours expense; and, I can answer for them, they had no views of any consideration for the great trouble they were at in collecting their materials together, more than the expectation of being in Madam's will, to empower them to receive each a legacy at her death.

I was by no means pleased with my situation. I was an utter enemy to distraction of all kinds, and had it not been for a nymph, who was a goddaughter of my aunt's, and lived entirely with her, I am certain I could not have rubbed through the month with any tolerable degree of patience. However, I observed my instructions, and though I could by no means give my assent to, I took particular care not to express my disbelief of the many ridiculous stories of ghosts and witches, which, with all the appearance of truth, were everyday repeated.

But this was nothing to the havoc made with reputations; many young maids were delivered in our parlour, who were absolute virgins, and, was faith to be given to these insinuators, there was not an honest wife or girl, of any tolerable person, in the whole neighbourhood.

But to the nymph—She was very pretty, about my own age, and excessively good-humoured; with a languish in her eyes, which seemed to tell her wishes extended to another sex. She was a great favourite of my aunt's, and would often merrily ask, What quarter she had to expect when she was absent? An answer was always ready, *When you do as they do, you must expect to be spoken of as they are.*

But we were even with them, and when we were alone, we gave them as little quarter as they afforded to others. In short, we grew very intimate, and I very foolishly made love to her. I, in my own thoughts, put her in the place of Chloe, and said, at every opportunity, every tender endearing thing to her I should have said to that idol of my mind.

This conduct was highly blameable, for it excited a real passion in her, whereas I intended only amusement to myself. I was glad to give vent to a passion which lay smothering in my breast, without ever considering she was susceptible to love, and I was about to do her an irreparable injury.

My aunt perceived our intimacy, and knowing she intended to leave her an handsome fortune, instead of putting a stop to such a dangerous intercourse, did more than we could desire to give us opportunities of being together. In short, we courted, kissed and toyed so much, and the poison so strongly operated, that one morning she surrendered to my importunity, and made me happy at the expense of her honour.

Honour! Where was mine! Where my faith, so lately renewed to Chloe! The impetuosity of my desires had banished, in a moment, honour, love, and Chloe from my bosom, and left me abandoned to lust—a slave to the basest of passions.

When I was alone, reflection stung me severely; pleasure was past, and the fleeting joy was succeeded by the pain of thought. In the midst of this distraction of my mind, the late innocent girl came into the garden to me—Alas! how changed! Instead of an open, smiling, good-humoured set of features which used to adorn, a dejection now overspread her face. The alteration was too visible to escape me; but reassuming some part of my wonted gaiety, I caught her in my arms, and told her as she had made me the most happy, she should find me the most constant of lovers.

I was obliged to do this to dissipate the gloom which hung upon her countenance, for fear my aunt should perceive it. Sighing she answered, *I must believe you—I will not doubt you—I have unhappily given you too much power over me.* Yet all my art availed very little—Notice was taken of her dejection; but, beyond my hopes, it happened it was imputed to a liking she had conceived for me, and, as it was imagined I had an equal one for her, my aunt endeavoured to persuade me to stay sometime longer, and she would undertake to prevail on my father to give me leave, adding, *I perceive you have engaged the affections of my god-daughter, and I can make her worth your having.*

I replied with encomiums upon the nymph, and my readiness to comply with everything she desired, but assured her, it would be in vain to apply to my father, as he expected to be punctually obeyed. But, if she wrote to him, she might express herself in such a manner as might induce him to consent to my returning at the end of the term. This she approved of, and, in about three days, having composed the unhappy fair one's temper, I set out, with a present of an hundred guineas from my aunt in my portmanteau.

CHAPTER XI

Contains Matters very extraordinary.

Immediately upon my arrival at Oxford, I discharged my debts, and established new credit, when my cash should be expended. I bespoke a laced waistcoat, and began to deviate from the statutable dress I had before observed. Such of my companions, who were resident, received me with great marks of esteem, and I began to grow very fond of myself. One day, after dinner, the tailor having executed his orders, I resolved to dress and made my appearance at a ball, which was to be that evening. Accordingly, about five o'clock, in a smart bob-wig, full of powder, a Baragon frock, a straw-coloured silk waistcoat laced with silver, black velvet breeches, white stockings, and new pumps, I sallied forth, flushed with my late success, and deliberately bent on conquest, but who was to be the happy fair was left to Chance.

This wild, aerial project, an unexpected incident crossed, and prevented my playing the fool in a place, where it is done with the worst reception in the universe. Just at the college gate, who should be inquiring for me but Mrs. Worthy's servant, who informed me his mistress and miss were at the Angel, and would be glad to see me.

What! Chloe in Oxford! Can it be, ye powers of love! Adieu ye Oxonian goddesses! ye imaginary beauties of thoughtless youth, adieu!—I was ready dressed, and quickly there, my heart beating time to my nimble steps.

The customary compliments being over, I learned from the good lady that as her daughter had been pretty much confined in attending upon her during her late illness, and had expressed some inclination to see Oxford, she had, to oblige her, made it in their way from Bath; and, as I was the only one they had any knowledge of, she had sent to desire the favour of me to accompany them, adding, she expected as much of my company as I could spare for the three days they proposed to tarry.

This was an agreeable employment to me, and I readily expressed my willingness to undertake it. But the execution of it was deferred 'till the next day. A year had so greatly improved Chloe, and given such a ripeness to her charms, that I viewed her with admiration. I had long thought it impossible for her beauty to receive the least addition—I could scarce think she was a mortal—I was struck with awe, and expressed myself the whole evening with diffidence, so fearful I was of offending. My vanity left me—I hated myself—I abhorred my desire of intriguing; and the sight of this dear girl at once recalled me to fidelity, honour, and herself. Such is the power of beauty when united with the force of virtue!

I retired after supper, ten the next morning being the appointed time to meet at breakfast. When I came to my room, my head was too full to think of going to bed. I traversed forwards and backwards a thousand times. I was in raptures at the thoughts of Chloe, but could not flatter myself with any romantic notion of how, when, or where I should possess her.

Though I had no reason to doubt her love, I was afraid her delicacy would not be brought to consent to do anything which might occasion a reflection upon her prudence. I started difficulties, and removed them. I formed many impossible schemes, and immediately the impossibility of executing any one of them rendered them abortive. I was in love, and ingeniously tormenting myself, and, at last, went to bed, steady to no resolution, except to trust all to her sincerity.

In the morning I attended before my time, and was so happy as to see Chloe come into the room without her mother. I saluted her, and expressed my joy at meeting her once again. She answered, *I am equally pleased; and, indeed, it was the hope of finding you here, which induced me to engage my Mamma to come this way.* I ventured to salute her again; saying, *My dear angel, allow this, to recompense the pain I have suffered in being from you so long.*

The coming of her Mother prevented any reply; and, as soon as we had breakfasted, we set out to visit the Colleges and public buildings, so universally admired. The adoration paid to her by the young gentlemen, raised my pride to the utmost pitch. Such admiration gave a sanction to my love, and all the public applause bestowed upon her, I interpreted as a public approbation of my passion. We returned to dinner, and I was glad to find they expressed themselves to be greatly pleased with what they had seen, which, at this walk, had not extended to above half of what they were to see.

After dinner, Mrs. Worthy addressing herself to me, said, *Sir, I must beg you to excuse me; for, since my illness, I have accustomed myself to sleep a little in an afternoon.* Upon that I offered to leave them, but she went on, *By no means, Sir; I do not confine my daughter: Oblige me by keeping her company. I will be down again by tea.*

Her absence gave me great satisfaction, and I observed to Chloe, this opportunity, so unexpected by me, gave me an earnest hope of my future good fortune: That as she had encouraged my love, something was due to it; saying, *My dear Chloe, you will go again in two days; and, if nothing is resolved on now, you will leave me in such an uncertain state, that I can have nothing to give me any ease, more than the remembrance that I have seen you. Seen you, indeed! more charming than ever! Thence springs my pain—I doubt not your word, but I would be out of the hazard of losing you.—What can I do?—What would you have me to do?* She replied: *You have my vows, you have my heart. You informed me, in your letter, you should be more at liberty.—You may see me often—give me more time—I will be constant to my promise— waive this discourse 'till tomorrow—I will do what I can, to make you easy.—But let me tell you the contrivance I made use of to give my letter for you, to your friend. I did not know what to understand by "Again tomorrow." However, I got my answer ready, and, at the usual time, was at the pump room. Your friend was there, and came close to me. He took out his snuff box, when, at that instant, I dropped my letter, saying, "Sir, you have dropped something." He took it up, and put it in his pocket, and I saw him no more after that day. Though we have been at Bath so long, I have been a close prisoner, except attending my mamma to the pump room. Fortune has hitherto favoured us —despair not.*

I had no reason to be dissatisfied with such a declaration, so chatted away the time 'till her mother returned to tea: After which I asked her, if she chose to visit one of the public walks? She said, *No, I am too much tired to go out again, but Chloe may take a turn or two, if she chooses it.* And her servant being called to attend her, we proceeded to St. John's, and found the gay and young of both sexes parading it.

Superior beauty claims superior respect. Chloe no sooner entered, than the male part of the company gave her due attendance. Wherever she went, they followed; and the nymphs of Isis were, this one evening, obliged to be witnesses of the inconstancy of their admirers. Our stay was but short, as her mother was alone; so we left the inconstants to their former contemplations.

This quick return was pleasing to her mother, and kept her from suspecting I had any inclination to be alone with Miss; and, indeed, I took the utmost care to be very circumspect in my conduct. I left them pretty early this evening, with an invitation to breakfast at ten the next morning; and, to my great satisfaction, found Mr. Trueman, my faithful friend, returned to College.

He had heard what a beauty I was showing the University to, and readily guessed who it must be, but that he thought proper to keep to himself. We concluded the evening, *tête-a-tête*, very agreeably. I went to my time in the morning, and, after breakfast, we proceeded to finish seeing the Colleges. I had forgotten to tell Chloe that my friend was returned, so that when we entered into our quadrangle, just before the bell rang for dinner, she was under some confusion at seeing him among the crowd who were gazing at her.

After they had seen what was curious among us, I took them to my room, which was put in order for their reception, and prevailed upon them to eat a slice of cold tongue and drink a glass of hock. Mr. Waring, that most excellent performer, entertained them with his violin.

Having gratified their curiosity by seeing everything, we reached the inn just as dinner was ready, after which her mother retired, as the day before, leaving us together, who, by consent, would never have parted.

We were no sooner alone than, looking tenderly at her, I begun, *My dear Chloe*—But she interrupted me, saying, *I remember my promise; but how can I keep it? It is a difficult thing you ask—what can I say?—Well, take your answer*, and, looking very grave, continued, *I am ready to give you every proof of my love—when I can do it with honour*; adding, with blushes spread over her face, *Contrive a way to marry me, and I will start no objections to retard it—I am yours.* Hear this, ye prudes! ye coquets! hearken; and all ye trifling idols, who love to torment!

I thanked her from my heart, and engaged to smooth the way to my own happiness—imprinting, with some courage now, several kisses on her charming lips.

Easy in our minds, and assured of each other's love, we wanted no third person to help to divert our time, which insensibly passed 'till her mother came to tea; at which, it was agreed to go to Woodstock the next day. Accordingly we did, and the following morning separated us once more; my dear Chloe going for their country house, and leaving me to pursue my studies. Mrs. Worthy, at parting, was pleased to tell me, if I ever came near where she was, she should take it unkindly of me if I did not spare time to call upon her.

CHAPTER XII

*Contains what passed between the Author
and his Friend.*

When the vehicle was out of sight, which seemed to hurry away my soul from my body, and was laden with all the treasure of my heart, I hastened to College to my friend. *She is gone!* I cried; the *charming creature is gone!—Pho, damn your whining,* he replied; *you have as much reason to be content as you can desire. Has she not been here? Have you not been with her? Three whole days with her! Does she not write to you? Are you not the happiest of mortals? Is she not beautiful as an angel? You are happy—I never can!*

His last words startled me. I imagined he loved her. He had seen her; that was sufficient to alarm me. *My dear friend,* says I, *what is the matter? Explain yourself—I can make nothing of this. Command me to the utmost, and you shall find I will undertake to serve you. Why then know,* he replied—*But she is lost!—irrecoverably gone!— When I was in London, I became acquainted with a pretty thing, an apprentice to a milliner—no matter where—she is gone forever.—I thought, from some polite airs she gave herself, how happy I should be in such a mistress—I attacked her* a-la-mode de *France; and, I assure you, as I did not offer her a trifle, by way of settlement for life, I thought myself in a sure way of succeeding. But my damned ill luck obliged me to go into the west, and, in my absence, a regular siege has been laid to her. I fir'd she has capitulated, a parson having witnessed to the articles. A jilt, to use a gentleman thus! Here, read the letter I had last night from our friend, Tom Atall—I entrusted him, in my absence, to manage the affair.* I took the letter, with great content to my own mind, and read as follows:

London,—

Dear Jack,

I have damned ill news to send you—
I'm an unlucky dog—but I did my best—When I found I could not get her for you, I tried for myself—but the same fortune—unlucky dogs both! A puppy of an haberdasher has bit us both—but dammee, I will have her yet, if I can; and so shall you—we'll snack her.—They tell me she values herself much upon her virtue, and all that, and will make an excellent shopwoman—never mind that—come to town—Revenge, I say.—The purlieus are all well.

Your Servant,

Thomas Atall."

Upon returning the epistle to him, he went on—*You will lend us your help—But, now I think upon it, you are driving for life, and Tom and I are for the whole sex—no matrimony, friend—though I hope sincerely your affairs go well.* Finding his disappointment had vexed him, I persuaded him to take a walk along with me; but he chose rather to ride, and came into so much temper, that he cried out two or three times *There are w—es enough—I am not fond of ruining a girl—but what business had she to give me encouragement?*

Our horses being ready, we trotted on towards Dorchester, and, by the way, he told me the whole that had passed between the young milliner and himself; in which I could find her no otherways culpable, than in admitting him into her company, after he had offered to bargain for her chastity. I used several arguments to persuade him from the resolution he had taken; and at length, after ome pause, he replied, *Faith, you are right—I wish her well—I will not concern myself at all about he — but I begin to want my dinner, let us push on a little faster.* We soon made Dorchester, and, to my great surprize, saw Mrs. Worthy's coach, with the wheelwrights hard at work in fixing a new axletree. *So, Coachman,* says I, *how do your ladies? Not much hurt, Sir; but it had like to have been an ugly job. They are at yon inn.*

As we passed the parlour window, to turn into the yard, Chloe knew me; and, getting from table, for they were just set down to dinner, came into the yard: *What brings you here?* says she. *Mere accident, Madam, I assure you. This gentleman and I only came to take an airing;* upon which my friend suddenly turning round, once more recalled the blushes to the cheeks of Chloe. *Pray come to my mamma,* says she; *we are just at dinner*: And introduced us with, *Mamma, here is Mr. A—and another gentleman.*

Her mother asked us, if we had dined? and, understanding we had not, insisted upon our sitting down with them. We were soon informed that the accident was occasioned by a farmer's servant heedlessly driving against the coach, in so rough a manner as obliged them to wait for a new axletree. We expressed our concern with hopes they had escaped without any hurt. *My maid is the greatest sufferer,* Mrs. Worthy answered; *her face is pretty much bruised. But it has been dressed, and she and I have been let blood. Chloe screamed, indeed, but that was all.* Mr. Trueman replied, he thought such careless fellows ought to be made examples of, and he was sure some of the people must know whose wagon it was. *Oh, Sir,* answered Chloe, *the farmer himself came to my mamma, and offered to make the damage good; but she would take nothing, only recommended to him to charge his servant to be more careful for the future. As we found we must stay two or three hours, my mamma thought it would be best to have a bit here, that we might not stop again 'till evening.*

It was a lucky accident for me, said a young lady, an entire stranger to me, whom I observed my friend to view with great attention. She seemed about fifteen, and, in any place without Chloe, would have been esteemed a beauty. The things being removed, Mrs. Worthy bid John call the coachman; upon his coming she asked him, how long it would be before he could be ready? He replied, *As soon as you please, Madam, for they have just done. We may reach Maidenhead tonight very well; or, if you choose to stay longer, Madam, there are very good inns at Henley. I would,* she answered, *be at London tomorrow evening; can you easily do that from Henley? Yes, Madam, if you please to set out sooner than you did this morning. Well, go and get your dinners, and in about two hours,* said she, *we will be ready.* Then turning to her daughter, she said, *Chloe, I will lie down a little; I am very sleepy after bleeding.*

Accordingly she withdrew, and left us to ourselves; when, addressing myself to the young stranger, *Pray, Miss, be so kind as to inform me how this accident is lucky to you? Why, Sir,* she answered, *I am at the boarding school here, and a letter came yesterday to my mistress ordering her to send me home the very first opportunity, for something, but what I am yet a stranger to, had happened in our family, which made my presence necessary; upon which my mistress sent to the inns, desiring to know if any coach would be going to London, and had room for one person. Being informed of this accident, she waited upon Miss's mamma, who very readily consented to give me a place in her coach. Lucky indeed! very lucky!* my friend exclaimed; *I think it really extremely lucky —else I had never seen you*: When, observing we turned our eyes full upon him, he awkwardly enough withdrew, saying to me, *Port is too heavy, I will order some arrack punch.*

Chloe immediately began to rally the young lady upon her conquest; but obligingly enough said, *You have no reason to be ashamed of it, Miss. He is a very pretty gentleman, I think.* I seconded it; and added, *I assure you, Miss, he has a very considerable estate, of which he will be in possession in about two months, being then of age*; and, observing her to be somewhat abashed, to give her time to recover herself, I followed after my friend.

I found him musing in the yard, and had no sooner got to him, than he caught me by the hand, crying out, *She is an angel! a perfect angel! you must assist me—your Chloe will help too—I am sure she will.* I assured him of my readiness to do everything he could desire; but said, *She is a stranger to me as well as you—a stranger too to Chloe.* He answered, with some impatience, *Chloe will know who she is, and where she lives, and all I want at present to know—Engage her to write you an account, and leave the rest to me.*

This I promised to do, and we rejoined the charmers. Chloe was seated in the window, the other was walking up and down the room. I sat down by Chloe, and, while he chatted with the other, told her the favour I had promised to beg of her. She heard me very patiently, and answered pretty loud, *I believe I may engage to do that.* However, the time of parting again drew nigh—her mother came down —Tea was soon over—the coach ready—and nothing left for us to do, but to hand them into it—and once more Chloe was hurried from my sight.

CHAPTER XIII

*Contains a Letter from Chloe.
The Author's Friend goes to London.
His Success; and other Occurrences.*

We returned to our bowl, and were no sooner seated than he began thus: *Forgive me, my dear friend, the folly I was guilty of this morning, and believe me incapable of ever thinking again of my milliner. Let me cry out with you, she is gone! the charming creature is gone! Ah! what an awful and becoming modesty was in all she said or did! What beauty!—what judgment!—pity me!—I love her, and must have her. I would give my fortune to stand as well with her, as you do with your Chloe. The world cannot match the pair! What a treasure does that coach contain!*

Thus he was going on, when, breaking in upon him, I told him, he had nothing to doubt; that Chloe had promised to give me the best account of her she could learn; that his fortune would smooth all difficulties, and enable him to demand her of her friends or guardian at once. *Fortune,* he exclaimed again, *shall be only secondary—I must have only love for love—no Smithfield bargain—let me hear from her own mouth she loves me.*

Thus he kept going on, 'till we were obliged to return to College; and, from that moment, he became the most altered gentleman I ever knew. Before, with many valuable qualifications, he was almost a debauchee; he now became serious, averse to wine in any excess, and expressed an abhorrence of his former favourite women of pleasure, ready to give up the whole sex, and willing to be called the husband of a girl of merit.

I was agreeably pleased with this turn, and told

him of the sentiments and commitments vowed between me and Chloe. He admired her generous conduct, and promised me his utmost assistance. In the situation we were both in, it will be no wonder we were inseparable.—On the fourth day came the letter, so much wished for by us both.

"*SIR*,   London,—

In part of the acknowledgment I owe to Mr. Trueman for his friendship to you, take the following account of Miss Schemal. She is the daughter of a gentleman, who has about five hundred pounds per year; but that goes to her brother, who is in the Army. She is a great favourite, for which reason her father lives very retired in——Street, near us, that he may give her a fortune. She ingenuously confessed, she might have about two thousand pounds; more she could not expect. Believe me, she is an incomparable girl, of a great deal of good sense, and much wit. I dare say her affections are disengaged. When we went to bed at Henley, I laughed at her about the conquest she made over Mr. Trueman. She answered me very freely, saying, She could not expect a man of such fortune. She hoped her papa would pay some regard to her inclinations, when he disposed of her; and, if so, *My dear Miss, give me the man I like, with a competency, rather than a coach and six, with an aching heart.*

"My mamma is so pleased with her, that she has recommended it to me, as her advice, to cultivate an acquaintance with her. The death of her mother was the melancholy occasion of her coming to town. I have been this morning to see her, and shall continue so to do, 'till decency will permit her to go abroad. My compliments to Mr. Trueman; I suppose you have made him your confidant—I will make her mine. You know my sentiments, in regard to yourself; they are still the same.

Adieu,

Chloe.

P. S. We go into the country in about a fortnight. I fancy my mamma stays so long to take Miss with her—I wish it may be so."

There, says I, tossing him the letter, *is an elaborate description for you to muse upon. I will go and order a bottle of wine, and toast my Chloe to you; you may find out a name for your favourite, against I come back.*

The wine being brought, *Here's Chloe to you—With all my heart,* he replied: *And now Lucinda to you.* Thus we went on 'till the bottle was empty, though not without considering maturely how to proceed. At last it was resolved he should go to London in a few days, and run the chance of seeing one or other of them in the park. This he put in execution, and it was my turn to wait with impatience his coming back.

Term grew towards an end, and I expected a letter from my father, with his leave to go to my aunt's, which came, and in a few hours after it my successful friend. He informed me that about eleven o'clock the morning after he got to town, he went and viewed both the houses, and narrowly made his observations which was the most likely way for them to go in their visits to each other, and fixed himself at a convenient place, with a resolution to attend the whole day, and every day, 'till he saw one or other of them. That the first day passed without success, but on the second, about half an hour after twelve, he saw them both go by, and followed them. That they went into *Hyde Park*, and bent their walk towards Kensington; upon which he hurried to Hyde Park Corner, and gave a coachman something extraordinary to make haste with him to Kensington Gate; that, as a servant attended them, the meeting might seem quite accidental.

The coachman, said he, deserved his hire, and I met them just as I could wish. I expressed my concern to see Lucinda in mourning, and said everything I was master of to convince her of my love for her; and I am greatly, nay, forever obliged to your generous Chloe for giving me all the liberty I could wish, never once interrupting me, but when she inquired after you. Lucinda answered me in general, She was too young to think of love: That she had a tender father, and would encourage no addresses without his consent.

I hinted my intention to be there again the next day, and how glad I should be to meet them, and found it was their common walk, being less frequented than St. James's Park. Chloe, with the greatest good nature, saying, "We were later to-day than usual." I left them at the head of the Serpentine River, as if I were going about business into Westminster. I had reason enough to be pleased with my success, but I could not bear the thoughts of applying to her father, 'till I was satisfied I was the person she truly loved.

I went to my friend Tom Atall, and found he had received a particular mark of his favourite's esteem for him, being in a deep salivation. I asked him how he had succeeded with the haberdasher's wife? but found, to my great satisfaction, he had no success there. I dined at a chop house, and frittered away the rest of my time in a coffee room where my face was unknown, 'till I went to my inn to supper and to bed.

The next day, about eleven, I repaired again to Kensington Gate. I had not waited long before I saw them coming, without any attendant. This pleased me, and I imputed it to the kindness of Chloe. The topic was the same—Love, pleading for indulgence; and, I thought, Lucinda seemed to be less indifferent, though she still continued to insist on doing nothing without her father.

I took my leave as before, but determined to give them the meeting the next day. They came to the same time as the preceding day; and Chloe informed me, she had been so happy, through her mamma's intercession, as to get leave for Miss to accompany her into the country, and they were to set out in two days. I pressed Lucinda earnestly to give me some encouragement, telling her, I should never think of making an application to her father for his consent, unless I had some reason to think it would be agreeable to her own wishes. "Well then," said your amiable girl, "Take my word you are not indifferent to her. Get her father's consent to court her, and she will consent to have you; we are not all giddy girls."—Is it so, Miss? May I flatter myself with so great an happiness? I said, addressing myself to Lucinda. She obligingly replied, "My friend betrays me, but I will not contradict her." I urged for leave to write to her, and, at last, obtained it.

Now, my friend, he continued, *you have had a minute account of all that has passed, except that I am charged by Chloe to deliver to you her compliments; and, by Lucinda, her good wishes—that dear girl saying, "Tell Mr. A—he is as happy as he need wish to be. I know all, and wish him success."*

I congratulated him upon his good fortune, saying, *There is nothing to retard your happiness but a little coy nicety, a few letters, a visit or two more, an application to the father, a settlement, and then, my good friend, your nuptials follow. You can publicly avow your passion, while I, if I am so happy as to get an opportunity to marry Chloe, must steal my joys like a robber, still contriving not to be discovered. This damps my spirits, and bangs a heavy weight upon my heart—This is the gall love mixes with my honey—But tell me,* I continued, *how do you propose to proceed? I am going to my aunt's, and should be glad to know your plan.*

To this he answered; *As I am just coming of age, I must visit my estate, to take possession, and make my neighbours drunk, according to an ancient custom in our family for ages: I then propose to call upon you, and we will proceed together to their country house. If Lucinda is in the same mind, I will wait upon her father; and, fixing upon Mrs. Worthy's house to be the first place I became acquainted with his daughter, tell him who I am, give him the particulars of my fortune, and ask her in marriage, for my temper will not bear delay; and, trust to my friendship, I will try hard to put you in possession of Chloe.*

CHAPTER XIV

The Author's Second Visit to his Aunt.

Within a few days I set out for my aunt's, my friend having first obliged me to accept of a very handsome horse. We parted with great reluctancy, but necessary business forced him one way, and peremptory commands compelled me another. For though my father was a man of great good humour, a good husband, and a tender parent, to all appearance, yet in everything he would be obeyed; and, if he once took a resolution, though without proper consideration, he was obstinately inflexible, and really deemed it a reflection upon his judgment to alter his mind.

When I came to my aunt's, I was received with great affection, but soon found I had a difficult game to play between my love for Chloe, and Corinna's (for so I will call my aunt's unfortunate god-daughter) love for me. When I proposed my father's leave to be obtained for me to return to my aunt's, I never once imagined he would comply with the request, any farther than to allow me to stay two or three days with her, in order to keep me in her mind, that she might remember me in her will. But I was mistaken, he had consented that I might come to her as often, and stay with her as long as she pleased.

This perplexed me—however, I resolved to be true to Chloe, and, as I really pitied Corinna, to let her fall as gently as was possible. I treated her with the utmost respect, avoiding every opportunity I well could of privacy—But her love was too violent to bear such usage—She told me one day, with some resentment, she knew of my gallantry at Oxford, and had heard a particular account of the beauty who robbed her of my heart—and, bursting into tears, said, *Yes, I am unhappy!—I am ruined! —Your cool behaviour convinces me of the truth!— but know, perjury never goes unpunished.*

I found I must alter my conduct, and to one falsehood add another. I told her, indeed I had conducted a pretty girl about the University, but my acquaintance with her 'till then had been very slight, having never been above three times in company with her before; that her coming to Oxford was purely accidental, as was my being there at that time; that her fortune was equal to a coronet, and it was reasonable to think her pride would not stoop beneath one; that as to my behaviour to herself, it was purely out of fear of the consequence, which might follow a more particular one; that my aunt, I was sensible, encouraged our mutual passion, but I believed would part with nothing 'till her death, and I was sure my father would never consent to my being married, 'till he knew how we stood as to fortune; that my behaviour deserved from her rather the name of prudent, than cool; that I suffered most, in being under such a restraint—*But*, said I, *no matter for the consequence, you shall have no reason to upbraid me with coldness;* and, catching her in my arms, was guilty again of treachery to the most generous and most beautiful girl the world ever knew.

Corinna was more ardent than became a young lady of her merit. She soon loosened her gown and divested herself of that garment and her uppercoat. In a trice she was stripped to her undercoat and I was free to gaze upon the treasures so ill-concealed by the flimsiness of the few garments she had left to cover her.

My eyes did not have to pry for the secret allurements: she untied her petticoat and let it fall around her feet; then inclining so slightly toward me she indicated with a gesture of her head that it was I who was to remove her shift. I drew it over her head, disarraying the curls that now lay in loose, untrammeled ringlets and fell softly at her shoulders.

Her breasts were small but veritable masterpieces of delight with their firm almond-shaped nipples shaded a delicate sunset golden-pink. And slender as was my Corinna, her flesh was of a stunning ripeness, all firmly fresh and succulent. My eager hands roamed hotly over the endowments Corinna had left in open display. Her breasts, her belly, that downy triangle beneath.

She motioned me to a couch. I saw that the girl was trembling. She reclined, shyly concealing her nakedness as best she could with her two hands. Gently moving them aside, I widened her thighs; I stroked that tender inner skin all the while whispering endearments. Moved by my heat, my fingers strayed to her rosy clit, stroking it assuredly, bringing it to a point of erection to match my own expanding member.

Thus emboldened by the answering breaths of the fair Corinna, I directed my fingers to the wellspring of pleasure. I separated the two outer lips presently closed tight. I made my entrance slowly so as not to distress the timid girl. Holding my probing fingers stiff, I guided them between the yielding, divided lips of the wound, and made my way past the initial resisting narrowness to that upper part, which widens out to receive the sensuous raptures.

Then pressing on with my quest, I lay my weight upon the outstretched figure and guiding my member with my still-damp fingers gently inserted it to the waiting lips. The slender sheath welcomed the entrance, enclosing my pleasure organ with warm embrace, duplicating the embrace which Corinna had fastened around my back with her arms and around my hips with her encircling thighs.

Slowly, to savour the sweetness of the tight embrace, I thrust and retreated. My engine, now encased in the valley of moist flesh, was engorged with the sensations of the highest delights.

I cried out, unable to contain my perceptions of bliss and Corinna answered with equal murmuring, thrusting her tongue into my ear. A roaring grew in my head. My thrusts grew ever more fierce and Corinna, inflamed with the hot juices of passion, moved rapidly to increase that sweet friction.

Behind my rod, past its shaft and down in the jewels which husband passion's liquor, I began to feel the hot surge of boiling liquid. The wave begins. Its momentum increases and our heaving and thrusting becomes more and more heedless. I was no longer the captain of my fate. The wave surged in me with a violence of its own. It thundered on, bursting out of the rigid head of my instrument with the force of hurricanes. Its crash on the shores of Corinna's receptive inner beaches was met with a shriek from the sweet girl herself, and writhings which fair tossed me from on top of her. It was only through the force of my own strokes that we stayed joined at the roots of our trunks for the exudations we emitted at the same instant.

I roused myself from that tender languor which follows passion and, bending to pay homage to those plump, lower lips, I saw draped from the wiry curls that surrounded them the pearly foam. Like the froth on a wave, it now was clinging about the outward edges of that ruby wound, so recently opened, which now glowed with a darker lustre following the unleashed passions we had spent on one another.

I licked that precious residue from its resting place. I then carried my mouth to Corinna's, observing the crimson glow upon her cheek, still flaming from the rush of blood heated by our mutual passions.

We dressed slowly, not wanting to shield from

each other's eyes the delights so recently tasted.

This encounter served well to fulfil our particular desires, and, too, to lay the storm at present: it dried up her tears; and, upon asking her who told her all her news? she readily answered, *A sweetheart of mine, a young Oxonian, Farmer Busy's son. And pray, Madam, how long have you been happy in his addresses?* I said, very seriously; *not that I ought to suppose your beauty could want admirers. Lard!* she replied, *what ails you? I hope you don't think—But I will tell you—about a year, at times; though I never encouraged him, I assure you. He came to my god-mother's the other day, and took an opportunity to tell me. He had heard your aunt intended to make a match between us; but, Miss, you will be mistaken, Mr. A—courts a young lady of great fortune, and she is with him now. I saw them together, when I came away. A fine creature she is! This is all, indeed;* adding, *I hope you are not jealous.* No, no, far from it; but, I believe, said I, *you think me greatly obliged to this tale-bearing, informing coxcomb. He did his endeavours to sow jealousy—I owe him my thanks.*

Matters being thus adjusted, and our amour renewed, Corinna resumed her pleasantry, and flattered herself she reigned sole mistress of my affections. We went into the garden 'till dinner, and, when we were summoned in, the young Oxonian, Mr. Busy, attracted by a good dinner, and the pleasure of talking politics uncontradicted, had taken his post at the table. He was unapprized of my being there. I knew him at first sight, but by sight only, remembering to have been shewn him by my friend Trueman, who once took a particular fancy into his head to kick him out of company for his impertinence.

He seemed a little chagrined at Corinna's serenity of mind; but, as he was not the most modest young man in the world, two or three glasses dissipated the very little he had. At length, being tired with his stupidity, I asked Corinna if she would take a turn in the garden? She answered in the negative, upon which I replied, *Well then, Miss, if you will not oblige me with a walk, I will oblige myself with a ride, my horse wants exercise*, and accordingly set out for a few miles. I was heartily vexed at the coxcomb, but knew not how to revenge myself.

On my return home, whom should I see but young Mr. Busy walking with a milkmaid; and, observing him to be very circumspect, I stopped by a thick hedge, and saw the pair retire to the side of a great haystack. I imagined he had used a great deal of rhetoric to draw the young thing into so private a place, but was at a loss how to turn the affair to my advantage and his shame.

While I was considering in what manner to proceed, a farmer-like man came riding by, and I thought proper, with Malagene in the play, to publish. We quitted our horses, and, coming softly to the other side of the stack, we heard the girl say, *Indeed I won't—If you love me, marry me.—I won't, indeed I won't. Pray, Sir, be civil. Zoons!* quoth the farmer, *that's my Jenny;* and, running round, he found the hot youth struggling with the girl to force her to a compliance—But the farmer soon cooled him, and having well disciplined him with his whip, permitted him to go about his business. The girl ran away, frightened half out of her wits, and left her pails full of milk behind her.

I was glad it was no worse, and went home, undiscovered by the amorous youth. I had the pleasure to hear the first gossip who came to our house repeat the story, but not the whole truth; for though I was a witness to the honesty of the girl, she was treated as a strumpet. The young Oxonian shifted his quarters, and sought out some place more propitious to his amours. The honest, unsuspecting part of the country, acquitted the girl of any intention to commit a lewd action, and she soon after became wife to a reputable farmer.

I acquainted Corinna with the whole transaction, and we made ourselves very merry at her lover's disappointment—She then informed me that after I was gone he told my aunt that he suspected me to be a young gentleman of very bad principles; that he was sure I was a Whig, and an enemy to the old constitution—*Well, well,* says I, *he will trouble this side of the country no more I am certain, either with his amours or his politics.* However, I heard nothing from my aunt about his principles; for I really believe she was so ashamed of his behaviour, that she judged him the most improper example she would wish me to follow, though she would have deemed me a monster, if she had in the least suspected my hypocrisy in one love affair, and my infidelity in the other.

CHAPTER XV

*The Author receives a Packet.
Corinna's generous Behaviour.*

When I parted with my friend I had directed him to address his letters to me at the post-house in—'till called for, and I began to grow uneasy at receiving no account from him. I was apprehensive too, from some expressions which fell from my aunt, that she had a mind to see her god-daughter settled before she died, and I knew she designed her for me. This required my utmost consideration. The consequence of refusing an old woman what she has set her mind upon, I knew was loss of favour. I knew too if I lost my aunt's, I should stand upon very indifferent terms with my father. He built much upon my being her heir, or, at least, co-heir with her god-daughter. This greatly disturbed me, but I had no remedy but patience. I was obliged to wait to see in what manner I was expected to act, before I could consent, or deny. However, I continued going to the post-house, and instead of a letter from him, I received a packet. The first I read was from Mr. Trueman.

"My good Friend,

I no sooner got into the country, than I wrote to Lucinda; and omitted writing to you, as I designed to be with you in person. I had an answer from the dear girl, with one enclosed to you, but when it came I was confined to my bed by a fever; a very violent one, I assure you, which was very near robbing me of my life and love. This was occasioned by my being obliged to do the compliments of my house in a more profuse manner, than agreed with my late regular life, so that I had not the letter for some days. I wrote a short answer, and kept your's, intending to bring it with me; but misfortunes seldom come single. I have put out my left shoulder by a fall from my horse, and it may be this fortnight before I can come; but you will have the satisfaction of receiving two letters from your Chloe, instead of one. I am more and more charmed with my Lucinda, whose second letter to me is expressed with some tenderness. This my illness, I imagine, drew from her, in spite of her reservedness. I will be with you as soon as possibly I can.

I am your most sincere Friend,

And humble servant,

John Trueman"

The others from Chloe were as follow:

"*SIR,*

Accept a line from Chloe. I was pleased with Mr. Trueman's coming to town, before Lucinda went with us into the country. I am sure he is not indifferent to her. He has written twice to her; the second letter frightened her—She burst into tears —*He is dying, my dear Chloe! he is dying!* It was well my mamma was retired, for I was terribly alarmed.—*Who? tell me, who?* says I.—She answered, sobbing, *Mr. Trueman!* and gave me the letter. I took her into the garden, and endeavoured to compose her, telling her, *Why you see he is recovered. Oh! but a relapse! my dear mamma died of a relapse.* However, at length she came pretty well to herself, and has written him a very tender billet.

Now to my own uneasiness—I am under strange fears—Here has been an old baronet five or six times with my mother, and very close they carry it. He gazes upon me with all the fondness of sixty-five. I am in the dark—I think my mamma will never marry again, but what business he has here so often puzzles me. Assure yourself however he is quite mistaken in Chloe, if he thinks the title of Lady will lure her into the arms of a dotard. You shall know more when I do, 'till when be assured of me.

Adieu,

Chloe"

"SIR,

The baronet has been very assiduous, and from some hints I found his aim was directed to me—. Yesterday the whole came out. A terrible battle Chloe has been in. My cousin came yesterday morning to my mamma, and they withdrew into her dressing room. In about an hour I sent for. Lucinda and I both imagined something very extraordinary was upon the carpet, by the secrecy it was conducted with. I no sooner was come into the room, than my mamma began; *My dear Chloe, I have always endeavored to treat you with the utmost affection, and, in return, you have been a very dutiful daughter to me. I hope you will continue so, and give me a proof of it by a ready compliance with what I am going to propose to you. Sir George Everyoung has had so good an account of your acquired accomplishments, and is so charmed with your person, that he offers an extraordinary jointure—indeed he offers a Carte Blanche for you. I have no exceptions to make, but I would have your consent; what you say, my dear Chloe?* I answered,

Madam, I cannot accept of the honour. I have endeavoured to be dutiful as far as I could, but this proposal I must refuse; and, bursting in tears, added, *Had I been undutiful, you could not well have contrived a greater punishment.* However, they battered me on both sides, my cousin being retained against me: But I stuck to my text—only I could not help throwing out some reflections upon my lover—*Does he want a nurse? He has daughters more capable of that office than myself. He will not part with his money in his lifetime, to marry them off; and he would settle a large part of his estate upon me, to rob them after his death*—*Chloe, Chloe,* my mamma said, *I give it to you as my advice—I will not compel you. Madam,* I answered, with some heat, *my dear papa recommended it to you not to compel me—I will not be compelled—I will not have Sir George, nor will I stay in a room with him in this house*: But, recollecting myself, I fell on my knees, and begged her pardon for expressing myself so warmly; upon which my mamma kissed me, saying, *Well, Chloe, it shall go no farther—dry up your tears—he is rather too old.*

You will not, I hope, attribute this conduct of mine to any regard I have for you—No, had my affection been quite disengaged, I never would have consented to have matched with such disparity of years. Lucinda compliments, and congratulates you —She commends me too.

Adieu,

Chloe"

When I returned home Corinna came to me, with great joy in her countenance, and told me, her aunt was going to write to my father for his consent to let us be married; and immediately perceived, by the alteration of mine, the news was disagreeable to me—*Be it so,* I replied gravely; *but assure yourself, Miss, the hour that such consent comes will be the last your eyes shall behold me. I cannot, Corinna, I cannot be yours—One unguarded minute has made us both unhappy. To dry up your tears I have already been guilty of hypocrisy to you, and infidelity to another. I know my ruin depends upon my refusal of you—but welcome be ruin. I was a villain to raise a passion in your breast—a greater to take advantage of it—Oh! that I could give back your honour, and take back my peace of mind! My vows, my honour, and my love are all another's—Farewell, I will abandon myself to fortune—Let fortune be my guide.—I pity you, Corinna; even now my heart bleeds for you. I would be just to you, but I cannot; Love will not suffer it. Farewell.* She caught fast hold of me, crying, *Hear me, I conjure you; stay to hear me. I want not your ruin—I am miserable!—I am guilty!—but I will not involve you in my guilt.—Stay with me, and I will hinder the match—I will break it off; or, at least, delay it—Believe me, I will; by the love I bear you, I will.*

She surely deserved my compassion, and I readily gave her my promise, that I would not go away, without her knowledge. When my aunt saw me, she said, *Well, Nephew, you must have my goddaughter*—I answered, *She did me a great deal of honour.* After dinner I withdrew, leaving them together, when she began the attack upon Corinna. Corinna replied, as she afterwards informed me, that she had the greatest obligations to her for bringing her up, and for her intended care in seeing her settled, but that I had never been particular to her: *The complaisance he has hitherto shown to me, I have imputed to his duty to you. I own, Madam, Mr. A—is very agreeable to me, but we are both too young, and I would be assured of his love to me, before I am so hasty as to give my consent, tho' I have no consent but yours to give.* My aunt answered, She did not intend we should marry yet, but she was willing to know my mind, that she might regulate her affairs accordingly.

It is easy to imagine with what joy I received this account from Corinna—My gloom cleared up —I admired her generosity, when addressing herself to me, she said, in a serious manner, *From this time, if you can, esteem me—give me a place in your friendship—All other liberties I forbid—I have no hopes now of having you, and I will not double my guilt—Keep my crime secret—I will mourn in secret for my life. May the mistress of your affections make you as happy, as I would have endeavoured to have done.* From this time I made her the confidante of my love, and we lived in perfect harmony, truly platonic both.

CHAPTER XVI

*The Author's Friend arrives.
They go to Chloe's Country-House.*

Corinna was charmed with my description of Chloe, ingeniously confessing she was a powerful rival, and her delicacy entitled her to the preference. This composure of mind in her perfectly composed my own. Two or three days after our scrub came running in, saying, *Sir, here is a fine gentleman, with two servants inquiring for you.* I immediately knew who this fine gentleman was, and had my aunt's permission to entertain him at her house. It is easy to imagine we were both sincerely pleased at our meeting. My aunt opened her cellar, the very best was allowed to his appearance, and proper care taken of his servants.

When we got by ourselves, we had enough to talk of—Lucinda and Chloe, Chloe and Lucinda were topics we could not be tired of: But I was obliged to satisfy him as to who the young lady was that dined with us. I told him she was designed for my wife, but I had made her an instrument of breaking off her own marriage, by ingeniously confessing to her I was, in affection, pre-engaged—that though a girl of fortune and great merit, so far from taking my confession as a slight, she generously had assisted me; and, if it was not laid entirely aside, it was like to be a long time before I heard any more of it. Filling a glass, he says, *Here's her health, and we will oblige Chloe and Lucinda to pledge it. Give me her name? Corinna to you, Sir,* I answered. Just then she came in, by my aunt's order, to see we wanted for no wine, or any liquor her cellar afforded. He charged another, and speaking to her, *Miss, pray pledge me; I have just drank your health, favour me with a glass to Miss Worthy.*

This was readily complied with, and with less confusion to herself than I could have imagined, addressing herself to me, *Sir, Miss Worthy, and happiness to you both. One favour more, Miss,* says he, *I have to beg of you; to drink Lucinda to me.—* This was done. *And now, Miss, I hope,* I said, *we may have your good company—we have no secrets.* Accordingly she went to my aunt, who, having two of the tale-bearing gang with her, gave her leave, and she immediately returned to us.

It was agreed for him to stay here three or four days, and that he should insist upon my going with him for about a week. He took an opportunity to slip a diamond ring upon her finger, telling me afterwards, it was intended as a trifle to Lucinda; but he was so charmed with Corinna's generous temper that he could not give it carriage any farther.

Corinna was faithful, and I found had apprized my aunt that the gentleman insisted upon my bearing him company across the country for a few days—*Aye! by all means,* my aunt answered; *I shall write to his father—The acquaintance of such a gentleman is not to be slighted.* Upon which intelligence, leave was soon asked, and as soon obtained, and we set out with great gaiety of spirits. But before we went, Corinna and I had some private conversation, in which she informed me how vastly pleased my aunt was with the present my friend had made to her, and that she desired me to persuade him to come back that way. Adding, *I see a particular pleasure in your friend and you; your horses, I am sure, will have but little rest, 'till you reach the place where your Chloe and his Lucinda reside—But let me conjure you not to make me your sport—sacrifice me not to mirth. I am unhappy enough—I will be your friend—I will never upbraid you.* My dear Corinna, I answered, *you have done so much more already than I could expect, that, believe me, you ever shall be mentioned with honour by me. I now repeat to you that if I could, I would be just. The report I made of you to my friend occasioned the present. I leave you, Corinna, with regret. Assure yourself you never shall be spoke of by me, but with encomiums upon your beauty, merit, and generosity.*

To my great satisfaction, she bore her fate with more resignation, than the mistresses of kings have done, though they fell adorned with titles, and the riches of kingdoms in their pockets.

She was certainly right in her conjecture, that we should make haste; and, indeed, we little more than baited, 'till we reached the inn we had agreed should be our headquarters. We invaded property, and the fences we could not leap, we broke through.

Here we came about seven in the evening, and, as we knew we could not proceed to business, inquired of our landlord, what company he had in the house? He said, there was one gentleman. We begged the favour of his company, and he readily complied. In putting the glass about, we found him an agreeable, communicative companion. He informed us, that he was an attendant upon the law; that about four months before he had contracted himself to a gentleman of great practice, and a great bird-fancier; that going the next morning to be set to work, the gentleman came to him, singing,

"*So they go up, up, up;*
 So they go down, down, downy;
So they go backwards and forwards;
 And so they go round, round, roundy."

Upon my desiring to know his commands; he replied, "By G—, he feeds himself;" and, turning from me, he went and listened to his nightingales, one of whom was making his first trial; and, hearing the bird go, Hoe, Hoe—"Dammee," he cried,

"*He's an Irishman.*" *I was a little surprized at the oddity of his behaviour, but, without taking any notice of me, he ran to the looking-glass, and after viewing himself with great attention, he exclaimed, "She is a fine woman!" Concluding him to be mad, I took up my hat, and left him without saying your servant.*

With these sorts of stories we amused our time, 'till we retired to rest. Our companion was proceeded on his journey, before we were stirring; and, about twelve, we set out for the residence of all we loved. Upon inquiring for Mrs. Worthy, we were showed into the parlour to her; when I began, *Madam, in obedience to your commands to call upon you, if I came near where you was, I have taken this liberty.* She very kindly replied, *Gentlemen, you are both welcome. I am very glad to see you. My family is at present in a little distraction; however, you shall not want a dinner. I was just going to visit the sick, but I will be with you presently.*

In the interim our minds were upon the rack—Those who love will feel for us—When Chloe came smiling in—*Gentlemen, I am yours.* My friend impatiently inquired for Lucinda, and was answered, She had been ill, but was out of all danger. This was a thunderbolt—*Come, Sir,* says Chloe, *be not dejected, we have taken the utmost care of her. Her papa left us but this morning, so you may be sure she is safe. I must see her, my dear friend; I must see her,* Mr. Trueman said, addressing himself to Chloe. She replied, *After dinner you shall, she sits up, but let me first apprize her of your being here,* which was judged to be very proper.

Many little endearments passed between Chloe and me, my friend walking up and down the room vexed at his cruel disappointment, as he called it; when, on a sudden, recollecting himself, he came gaily up to us, and taking each of us by the right hand, and joining them together, obligingly said, *There are, except my Lucinda, none so dear to me as yourselves. Your affections are joined, I join your hands for the present; and insist, Miss, upon being your father, when they are joined forever.* She blushing promised he should, saying, *I know my conduct will be censured—I cannot help it—But my heart approves it. Old people may talk of subjecting love to reason, I experience young ones cannot. Fairly spoken, Miss,* he replied, *though, in my opinion, you have acted with reason, if birth and merit can lay any claim to beauty and fortune.*

Her mamma's appearance put a stop to any farther discourse of that sort; and, dinner being served up, we were several times told by the good lady, she took our visit very kindly: *We have been,* she added, *in some confusion, but I suppose my daughter has informed you. I acquainted Miss Schemal what company I had unexpectedly come. A little company will divert her.* In about an hour after she withdrew; saying, *Chloe, when I ring, show the gentleman the way.*

We admired the good nature, the friendly disposition of this gentlewoman. Pride she was a stranger to; good she did to all she knew to be in distress. She loved her daughter, and wished her a title. If she had a foible, it was that of being anxious for her advancement in the world, as she termed it. She would have sacrificed, had it been in her power, her daughter's present fortune, and her own estate besides, to have obtained her a title; and, so her daughter had been a lady, she would have been at little pains to have examined into the merit of the person who honoured her with the title of ladyship—Hence sprung the secret treaty with the old Baronet. Excuse that one foible, she was a woman without fault.

The bell rang and I said to Mr. Trueman, *My dear friend, be careful how you act.* We were showed into Lucinda's bed-chamber, and, after a few compliments bestowed upon her, Mrs. Worthy retired, saying to me, *Sir, you know my custom; I treated you with the same rudeness at Oxford.*

Glad at my heart I was she was gone, for she was no sooner out of the room than Trueman flew to his Lucinda, kissed her, and expressed his happiness in finding her recovered. *What should I have done had I lost thee! How happy am I to find you well, ere I knew you had been ill!*

My imagination suggested to me, it would be proper to acquaint Mrs. Worthy with the whole affair. Chloe approved of it; we communicated it to our two friends, and received their approbation. Mr. Trueman, looking at me, said, *I have forgot myself*; and, turning to Lucinda, *one glass of wine will do you no harm.* She answered, *I believe not. Come then, we will drink a health to Corinna.* This name was unknown to either of our favourites, and we observed they looked at one another with some astonishment. Who is she? was the question we saw each wanted to ask. But my friend soon eased them, by acquainting them with the whole affair. Chloe, with great pleasure, said, *With all my heart, I will drink her health. She has acted beyond her sex*—Lucinda threw in her commendations. *I think it would be right,* my friend said, *when Chloe tells her mamma of my love for you, to say Mr. A—is going to be married to Corinna. It will entirely banish all suspicion, and give him opportunities to converse with her at more liberty.* As I was in civility bound to call at Lieutenant Colonel Standard's, we took our leave, with a promise, we were sure to keep, of coming again; and, leaving our compliments for the good lady of the house, we departed.

CHAPTER XVII

*Treats of Some Things before the Author
was born, and others afterwards.*

We were received with great complaisance, and pressed to stay there, the Colonel saying it was no inconvenience to him at all; that he had a field the horses might run in, and they should not want for corn; *Nor you, Gentlemen, for plain diet and good wine.* I kindly thanked him, but, as we were only upon a tour, my friend had obliged me to promise him, I would not trouble any of my acquaintance, with putting them to the expense of entertaining him, two servants, and three horses; as it was more than probable, he should have no opportunity of returning the compliment at his own house. This excuse passed. Mr. Trueman said, *Sir, we propose to stay at our inn about a week, and, as we may probably call upon you often in the time, I hope you will so far favour us, as to give us your company to take a bottle there. I promise you*, he answered, *Gentlemen, I will. I have a great regard for my young friend here: His father and I have been in several engagements abroad, and he has exerted the spirit of his father in the protection he gave to a young beauty in our neighbourhood; and I hope, will exert it equally, if there be occasion, in the service of his king and country.*

The Colonel ordered his horse and rode with us to our inn, and we were greatly pleased with the company of a gallant old officer.

When we arrived at our inn, who should we find there but young Mr. Busy. On either side good manners passed. He chose to stay out of fear we should talk of him in his absence—A theme below us! We chose he should stay, as I was sure the Colonel was an over-match for him, if he should start any more of his usual discourse. He inquired of me, with great confidence, concerning his friends on our side the country, and I gave satisfactory answers. Mr. Trueman ordered a very handsome supper, and sent in a bowl of punch.

When we were seated, I took the liberty to ask young Busy, how long he had been on this side the country? *About three weeks,* he answered; *and this afternoon I have been to pay a visit, my first, indeed, to a gentlewoman in the neighbourhood, one Mrs. Worthy. I think I saw the same young lady there, who was at Oxford with you. She is her daughter I find.* (Consummate assurance! I thought) *It is a very pretty retirement. We dined there,* said Mr. Trueman. *Very possibly,* he replied. We had a pretty warm dispute between the old officer and him after supper. When it was near ended, Mr. Trueman, in order to change the subject, *With your leave, I will toast Corinna,* addressing himself to me. Young Busy immediately replied, *Aye, Sir, there is a girl with money too, to make her go down.* I will not die in your debt, I thought. The next toast was his; and he very modestly gave Miss Worthy. *Aye, Sir,* I cried, *there is a girl with money too, to make her go down!* I gave Miss Jenny, the farmer's daughter—*A very pretty girl,* quoth Busy; *I have seen her.* (Impudence to perfection!) *Indeed,* I answered, *she is very pretty, but her father is somewhat rough, is he not so, Sir? I know your meaning,* he replied; *you jeer me, but there are none who are not subject to scandal.*

We called for another bowl, and pipes and tobacco; and the Oxonian modestly, for the only time in his life, withdrew. The old Colonel wondered at his impertinence, to toast a young lady he never was in company with but once, and in the very parish she lived, concluding, *If he goes on so, his familiarity will oblige him to decamp.* We finished our evening in pretty good time, and, insisting upon the Colonel's lying at the inn, we respectively adjourned to our apartments.

CHAPTER XVIII

*Contains various Matters.
Mr. Trueman is taken ill, etc.*

The first salute I had in the morning was, *You lazy creature, would you lie all day?* This was from the Colonel; upon which I immediately got up, and we roused Mr. Trueman. He complained, he was not very well, but he did not know what ailed him. We passed it off, and walked down to my friend's to dinner. His family consisted of himself, a housekeeper, two maids, a footman or groom, and a gardener.

The old gentleman made me smile two or three times—*You are not here,* says he, *for nothing. I remember, young gentleman, when your mother was carried off.* This was a secret I was unacquainted with—It startled me, and I begged him to inform me. *Not yet,* he replied; *you shall know all in due time. But, tell me, who is to be the happy youth? I smell a rat. Sir,* said Mr. Trueman, *it would be an ill compliment to you, not to trust you with any secret we have. We are, I hope, both to be the happy youths*—and discovered the truth.

The Colonel looked very seriously at me, and then gave the following account—*Your father, Sir, is a gentleman I value. He is a man of courage, has great merit, and great foibles. Your mother is of a distinguished house in England—you are no stranger to that, though, possibly, you will be to part of my story. He fell in love with her, and attempted everything man could do to make her sensible of it. He had then only a company, and has never had more than half-pay as Captain, from the time the Regiment was broken. His marriage, instead of making, hindered his preferment. Your mother gave him encouragement, and, when we were to march out of the place, she met me, according to an agreement between them, and I concealed her in a baggage wagon, giving the Sergeant of that guard positive orders to let no person get into that wagon. I overtook the wagoner, and ordered him to turn up to a little village, within a quarter of a mile of the road—There was your father with a licence, and there they were married; and, begging your pardon, Sir, in a hedge-alehouse they bedded. To be short, a hue and cry followed Miss, but before she was found, she was a wife. This had like to have occasioned bloodshed; but they came too late, and out of regard to the family she came from, they settled six hundred a year upon her, for her life only, and have taken every step since to prevent your father from being promoted. You will excuse me, Sir, for being so free. If your mother dies, I know your father—You are sure of two thousand pounds, left you by the most generous relation of your mother's side.—As to the young lady, who, it seems, favours you, she will, if she out-lives her mother, or marries with her consent, be worth about two thousand pounds per annum. I might say more, as their whole fortune is in the stocks, and pays no tax.*

This account struck me all of a heap—A beggar to pretend to Chloe—What are two thousand pounds? They perceived my dejection, and endeavoured to cheer me up; however, I secretly resolved to tell her the whole truth. I was angry with my father for keeping so material an affair hid from me. My sentiments were then so just, that, had I known it, I should never have opened my mouth to her concerning love. We passed the day indifferently enough to me; and my friend continuing to complain he was not well, we returned early in the evening to our inn.

The next morning we walked down to Mrs. Worthy's, to inquire after their healths. Chloe had discovered Mr. Trueman's love for Lucinda to her mother, and informed her of his fortune: She seemed mightily pleased; and, when we came in, after the usual ceremony, she said to my friend, *Sir, I approve your choice—She is a very deserving young lady—You intend, I find, to wait upon her father for his consent—I will write to him myself, and, if you please to give me a letter, I will enclose it in mine—My recommendation shall not be wanting:* Then addressing herself to me, *Sir, here have been tell-tales too about you—Well, you have my good wishes—I wish you all happy.*

When she had done speaking, with great good nature she took Mr. Trueman by the hand, and led him out of the room to Lucinda's, leaving Chloe with me. She acquainted me, that after we were gone, a young Oxonian came in, and had prevented her telling her mamma anything about me, by doing it for her—*I know who it was*, interrupting her; *I had the honour to drink your health in his company the same evening. I hope*, she answered, *you have not been guilty of such an indiscretion, as to toast me in company. No indeed*, I replied, *but he has, if it is an indiscretion;* and, looking very serious, *my dear Chloe, favour me so far as to go with me to the bottom of the walk—I have something to say to you, that is material you should know.*

When I had discovered the whole to her, she replied, *If my esteem for you could bear increase, this honesty would increase it—I set not my love at a price—neither six hundred nor six thousand a year can buy it—I gave it to you, and your loss gives me pleasure—I am glad to have this opportunity to tell you, you only can make me happy. You were disinterested when you offered me your heart; I accepted of it, and, to convince you I am as disinterested as you, whenever you please I will be yours.*

This answer received the utmost thanks a grateful mind could bestow, and, returning towards the house, Mr. Trueman met us. *Sir*, Chloe said to him very gravely, *could you imagine your friend capable of abusing me? but I deserve it; my easy compliance merits such usage. Not to keep you longer, Sir, in suspense, he has conceived so mean an opinion of my love, as to think I am so mercenary a creature, as to barter it for six hundred a year; and, finding he cannot purchase it, he wants to throw it upon my hands again.* He perceived her meaning, and answered, *I commend him for not concealing his circumstances from you, Miss; and I will do him the farther justice to assure you, he has acquainted you with them almost as soon as he knew them. Phoo, Phoo,* she replied smiling, *you two always praise one another—But I have punished him—I have obliged him to take me whether he will or no.*

This brought us to the parlour door, and respectfully taking our leave, we went to our inn to dinner, having been obliged to promise the old officer to dine with him the next day.

In our way, my friend told me, Chloe's mother carried him to Lucinda, and had obliged him to write a letter to her father, telling him, she chose to surprize people with good news.

The next day at noon we returned, according to our words, though with some reluctance on the part of Mr. Trueman; he saying, *I continue ill, and shall be but indifferent company—but, to see Lucinda, I will go.* He eats very little at dinner, complaining much of his head. In the afternoon, the apothecary who attended Lucinda came in, and was immediately desired by Mrs. Worthy to look at him. Accordingly he felt his pulse, viewed him and then said, *Sir, you are very feverish; I would have you go to bed.* Mr. Trueman replied, *Sir, I am at such an inn, I will go presently, be pleased to give me your attendance. I will just, Madam,* addressing himself to Mrs. Worthy, *speak to Lucinda, and do as I am advised.*

He was no sooner withdrawn, than Mrs. Worthy said, *Chloe, order a bed to be got ready; no gentleman shall go sick out of my house to an inn*—and asked the apothecary what he thought was the matter with him. *Why, indeed, Madam,* he replied, *the gentleman has got a very dangerous fever.* This threw us all into confusion, but I begged of her to say nothing to him; but, as she was so obliging as to insist upon his being at her house, I would get him to bed, and would leave it to her or Miss to break it to Lucinda.

When Mr. Trueman returned, Mrs. Worthy said, *Sir, you are not to go out of the house—An inn is an improper place—I have ordered a bed for you.* He thanked her, and I attended him to it, while the apothecary went to fetch what was proper. He was no sooner in bed than he insisted upon my telling him what the apothecary thought of him. I told him the truth—*I expected no less,* he said, *from your friendship. I am not any way afraid; but I will make my will, for fear of the worst. I must show Lucinda how much I value her, and you shall know how high you stand in my esteem. Take these bank-notes into your custody—I give them to you—I shall want nothing here. Let my servants stay where they are, and I beg you to acquaint Lucinda with my illness.*

I went and told Mrs. Worthy what he said, who immediately sent for her lawyer; and, a will being drawn to his mind, it was properly executed. I asked, and had his leave to send one of his servants to my aunt's; but the difficult part of my commission was yet to do. I begged Chloe to go with me to Lucinda's chamber, and she immediately asked where Mr. Trueman was. I told her he was not very well, and was laid down; and, by degrees, let her into the truth. We could scarce prevent her running to him, but at last prevailed upon her to stay for a few days longer in her room, solemnly assuring her, she should know the very worst, and that we would conceal nothing from her.

I then went to the inn and acquainted his servants, sent one to my aunt's with a letter, and hastened back to him. I set up with him every night, 'till he was out of all danger, going to bed for a few hours in the day. Lucinda was at length suffered to visit him, and expressed herself very tenderly upon his illness.

He recovered pretty fast, and said one day to Lucinda, as she sat by his bedside, *One disease I am cured of, but when will you set about to apply a remedy to the other? All in good time,* she replied; *but let us hear what my papa says, not a step farther without his consent.*

In the meantime the servant returned from my aunt's, with an account of all being very well. Corinna wrote me word my father had sent an answer to my aunt, such as I could wish; expressing himself with a great many thanks for her favours to me: But he could not consent to my being married yet—it was too soon to settle for life—and had concluded with giving her leave to do by me as she pleased, a few years hence; with his wishes she might live to see them, and many more. Corinna added, *My aunt is not very well pleased, tho' I am sure you will, with his complimental denial: However, she expresses no manner of resentment to you; but, on the contrary, great kindness.*

The term drew on, and it was necessary for me to think of returning to Oxford. Chloe's mother and Mr. Trueman were very uneasy at receiving no answer from Lucinda's father. Chloe and I were as happy as we could wish, having all the opportunity we could desire to express our mutual passion. At last the wished-for letter came. He expressed himself highly obliged to Mrs. Worthy for the care she took of his daughter, and was very sensible of the honour Mr. Trueman did him; but he could not tell what to say, as to the intended courtship—An extraordinary accident had happened, which rendered him incapable of giving Lucinda the fortune he had saved for; the person in whose hands it was being gone off with that, and many thousands belonging to others—*But, Madam,* he concluded, *I submit it to your judgment, and leave her to your discretion.*

This was communicated to Mr. Trueman, but concealed from Lucinda. My friend said, *Madam, my intentions are honourable—My fortune is more than sufficient to support us splendidly—I cannot live without her—I ask for none, nor do I expect any fortune.* She answered, *Then, Sir, I give you permission to make your addresses to her, and I will tell Lucinda she is at liberty to receive them.*— I set out for the University, and once more was separated from Chloe.

CHAPTER XIX

*The Author receives an Account
of the Death of his Mother.
A Strange Revolution in the Family, etc.*

I called at my aunt's, purposing to stay there three or four days. Corinna and I met with our passions as much subdued, as if they had never been rebellious. I observed, indeed, a melancholy preying upon her, and she seemed to give it entire indulgence. I said all I could to divert it, but to little purpose. She assured me, she had entirely divested herself of her love, and all thoughts of me, farther than her esteem and friendship: *But I have cause,* she said, *to grieve; my days I dedicate to sorrowful reflections, and my nights to tears.*

I was sincerely sorry to see her in this way, and began to be affected with her malady, and to sympathize with her in her melancholy. I knew myself to be the cankered worm that ate at the roses from her cheeks—I loathed myself. Being obliged to proceed on my journey, I earnestly recommended to her to take care of her health. She shook her head, saying, *When I cease to think, I shall cease to mourn.*

I passed my time as usual, between my exercises and my friends, when one day I received a letter from my father. The contents were melancholy enough—my mother, I found, was dead, and he must lead a retired life—He should be glad to see me always, but I must not expect him to do anything more than give me his blessing and pray for me—That I had two thousand pounds, which was at interest in such hands, at four percent; and he would give me a proper power to receive it.

So then, I thought, the blow is come at last; but how heavy would it have been, if I had not been before apprized of it?—To be stripped of six hundred pounds a year, at one dash of a pen, would have been a cutting stroke: However, I pulled up my spirits, and bespoke mourning, intending, when term was over, to visit my father, and pay my duty to him. I considered him as acting generously by me, to trust the money to my own management.

I wrote him a letter, full of all the dutiful expressions I could think of, and soon after received another from him, with one from the gentleman whose hands the money was in, letting me to know he would pay the interest to my order, and if I wanted the principal, the condition he took it upon was to have six months notice, and to such notice he would pay it to me.

At the end of the term I set out, and immediately, upon my arrival in town, went to wait upon my father. He received me very affectionately, but said he did not expect to see me without his orders —That he perceived I had ridden up, and he was glad of it, as he had no bed for me, the furniture being removed to a less house, and what he should not want was to be sold; but where my horse was, I might lie.

I confess I was not over pleased with my reception, especially as two or three days passed, and I was not made acquainted where this less house was. I inquired of the porters where they carried the goods to, and was answered to Mr. Clinch's, a broker—However, the whole came out at last, and separated my father and me for life.

I was going from my inn one morning, and casually met with my mother's late maid. She accosted me with, *How do you do, Sir? I hope my master is well. How do you like your mother-in-law?* I answered her, she told me news; I had seen no mother-in-law, nor did I know I had one. *Lard!* she cried, *that is strange, my master has been married these ten days.*

103

With a little importunity she informed me that my father was married to a widow with a pretty jointure, with whom he had kept company some years, and had two children by her, adding some other intelligence that greatly displeased me— Then dropping me a curtsy, with, *Sir, I am glad to see you*, away she went.

The regard I had to the memory of my mother drove all the duty I owed to my father from my breast; and, returning directly to my inn, I took horse for Oxford, without giving him the least notice of my departure.

I was astonished, when I came to reflect upon his conduct—A man so regular, to all appearance, in his way of life; so seemingly fond of my mother; so outwardly good, and so inwardly bad—Yet he was my father, and I was sorry for my precipitate resolution, though, at the same time, I determined never to go near him again, unless he sent for me— which he never thought it worth his while to do.

I now looked upon myself as my own master, as indeed I was, and resolved to stick more close to the University, as being the cheapest place I could well stay at, 'till fortune should give Chloe to me— to make frequent, but short visits to my aunt's, with a view of keeping her in the humour of sharing her fortune between Corinna and myself. These certainly were good resolutions.

I had near three hundred pounds, which my friend gave me when he was taken ill, and which I could not prevail upon him to receive again, he saying, *It was a trifle for the attendance I had given him*. Accordingly, I divided my time between the dead, the present, and the absent—some part of the day I allowed to books, some part to my companions, and the other to my contemplations upon Chloe, Lucinda, Corinna, and Mr. Trueman— When a letter came from him, as I thought, by the direction; but, upon opening it, it was from Chloe.

"SIR,

"Our friend is so taken up with idolizing his Lucinda that I cannot get him to spare time to write to you, so accept of the agreeable employment myself. Lucinda's father has been here, and mightily approves of Mr. Trueman for his son-in-law, not, he has assured us, through the consideration of his estate, but in regard to his good qualities. She is as handsome as ever, and he perfectly recovered. Mr. Trueman informed me of the death of your mother. He was told it by our neighbour the Colonel, and of your father's sudden marriage—I condole with you. We have been visited too by Lucinda's brother; he seems a pretty gentleman, but took more notice of me than I could wish. My cousin brought here too, the other day, the 'Squire, who gave rise to our intimacy. He begged my pardon, and had it. He has called here twice since, and my cousin has been very busy with my mamma. The wedding is to be when we come to town, and our friends agree and insist upon your being present. There will be no one else at it, but myself and her father. He is a very agreeable man, about my mamma's age, and, I believe, would like her very well for a wife—but I do not think she will marry again. I wish I have not got two lovers; but you need not doubt me, though there were twenty. If you do not come this way before we come to town, you shall hear again from me. Mr. Trueman will direct my letters—Your answer must be to him. We pass our time very agreeably; and, I assure you, my mamma drinks the health of Mr. Trueman's friend every day. I hope Lucinda will be true to me, yet I almost wish I had not trusted her with our secret. Your friend is true to your interest; but he is a man, and capable of friendship. Lucinda is of another sex, and has a brother she loves dearly. Accept their compliments.

Adieu.

Chloe."

There were hints enough, in this letter, to let me see her constancy must endure some trials, and I was farther from possessing the dear girl than before. Rivals have quick eyes—but I was forewarned. The 'Squire, I knew, had a very great estate; and Chloe had nothing to object to his years, as she had to the Baronet's. As to Lucinda's brother, I was sure Mrs. Worthy would never give her consent to him, no more than she would to me, except his father and she should make a match, and then what might be hatched in a warm bed I could easily foresee. I found we were both likely to have business enough upon our hands, and I at once resolved to do nothing rashly. I knew the sincerity of Chloe, and upon that I rested; but I judged it proper to draw nearer the enemy.

CHAPTER XX

*The Author goes to his Aunt's,
and to Chloe's.*

Before I set out, I wrote two letters, one to Mr. Trueman, and the other to Chloe—as follow.

"*My good Friend,*

Chloe made your excuse for not writing to me. I accept of it, and am happy to know you are so well employed, and all your fears over. She invites me to the wedding—I will come, as well-pleased guest, to see the nuptial-knot tied. I am just going to pay my devoirs to Corinna; but when my nuptial-knot will be tied, I do not know. I will detain you no longer; only assure you,

I am yours sincerely."

"*Dear Chloe,*

I am sorry to find you are likely to be subjected to more importunity than you desire, though it is no more than I expected—Such beauty could not fail of attracting admirers. I am coming to my aunt's; and, very possibly, shall make it my business to come farther. I can give you no advice; I am afraid, if your mother should marry, you will be more uneasy upon the Captain's account, than the 'Squire's. I cannot think Lucinda will take part with her brother against me and Mr. Trueman. Out of regard to him, I conclude, she will rather be indifferent: However, I am perfectly easy as to yourself. They may tease you, but they cannot compel you to marry.

My dear Angel,

Adieu."

These being dispatched, I set out. I found my aunt in mourning, and she soon let me know she had heard of my father's marriage—*Hasty work indeed!* she said; *before one wife was cold to get another! Pray have you seen your father and his bride?* I answered, *I had seen my father, not her;* and gave her an account of my reception, and my coming away. *You have done right—You are welcome to come here when you will,* she replied. *But pray put this girl into better humour; she is so eat up with the vapours, we do not know what to do with her. She is the daughter of a man I once loved, and the only one I loved; but our friends crossed our inclinations, and we could not venture to trust to live upon love alone, as not being sure they would ever forgive us, if we married without their consent; and he, tired of waiting for me, made his addresses to another, and married her. I could not bear to see him for years after; at last I stood god-mother to this girl, their tenth child, and the only one left. He ran through all, and died just time enough to keep out of a jail. I took this helpless orphan, have brought her up so far, and I should be sorry to lose her now.*

She spoke this with so much affection that the tears stood in her eyes. I applied myself assiduously to my task; and whether it was, she believed I had not slighted her through any distaste, or from my being with her, but she re-assumed a good deal of her usual cheerfulness—and I saw, with pleasure, the roses reviving upon her cheeks. My aunt was equally pleased, and said to her one day, *My nephew has met with a great loss in his mother; but, when he has finished his studies, and fixed upon his way of life, I will see you married, and die contented.* I was fearful, as she knew I depended so much upon her, she would have exerted her authority, and fixed upon a shorter day.

I communicated Chloe's letter to Corinna, saying, *My dear Corinna, my love has hitherto gone smoothly on; but the clouds are gathering, I must feel a little before I can be happy. Had I never seen Chloe—Had I not been engaged to Chloe—You would have reigned sole mistress of my heart—The only object of my love.*

Thus with a good design, and with a good effect, I soothed the unfortunate Corinna. I told her of my intention to visit Mr. Trueman, but that I would not stay there above a day; and, acquainting my aunt where I was going, I once more proceeded to Chloe's—But I first called upon my good old friend the Colonel. He received me cordially; and, upon my telling him what I came about, he answered, *Aye, Aye, young gentleman, you must look about you, your favourite is hard beset.*

When I came to Mrs. Worthy's, Mr. Trueman saw me ride up to the gate; and, running out to me, *My dear Friend,* he cried, *you are welcome—Chloe is a girl of spirit. Come in, come in;* and, taking me by the hand, hurried me into the dining room, without giving me leave to ask him one question.

I found myself in a large company, and, making my obeisances, sat myself down. Mr. Trueman said, *This is kind; I thought you had forsook the country, and forgot your friends.* I answered, I never forgot them; but my aunt, since my father's marriage, had confined me very much, and I was now obliged to promise to return almost immediately, before I had her consent to come. *Very well, very well,* he replied; *but Corinna is the lodestone that attracts you there. How does the fair charmer? I am told she is very pretty,* said Mrs. Worthy. *She is indeed, Madam,* young Busy answered; who, having a strong liking to a good table, made frequent visits to the most wealthy of the neighbours.

By this time I had discovered my company, and found it to consist of Lucinda's father and brother, the 'Squire, the cousin, young Busy, Mrs. Worthy, Mr. Trueman, the two beauties, and myself; and I observed, with some concern, Lucinda was not so open in her expressions to me as usual. She seemed to affect a good-natured way of speaking; however, I imputed it to the presence of her father, and behaved with the same open freedom I had ever accustomed myself to.

The 'Squire and the Captain, I saw, regarded each other as dangerous rivals. The Captain was afraid of the 'Squire's estate; and the 'Squire afraid of his gay dress, his easy address, and his long sword—Lucinda's father was very particular to Chloe's mother.

I soon perceived it would be impossible for me to have any private discourse with Chloe. I had only the pleasure of observing, she treated the 'Squire with bare civility, and the Captain with very great indifference.

Sometime after dinner, to amuse themselves, cards were called for. *Well, I think,* said Mrs. Worthy, *you must cut in, and then no notice can be taken of any preference. My cousin and I will go into the little parlour to backgammon. And I, if you please, Madam,* like Lucinda's father said, *will go too, and take up the conqueror.* I excused myself, on account of my time, and the promise I had given to their neighbour to come to him again; saying to my friend, *Sir, to inquire after your health, and the family's was the sole occasion of my coming; and, as I am so happy as to find you all well, I will keep true to my promise to my aunt, and get back as soon as I can. I will go with you to the Colonel's,* Mr. Trueman replied. *He is a gallant man. We will walk down—My man shall bring you your horse: So there will be but five to cut in—I mean only three—the ladies must play.* Chloe answered, *Fair play is fair play—I will take my chance* —and was cut out. *I hate to look on,* she said; *and, if you please,* looking at my friend, *I will take a walk with you. With all my heart,* he answered; *come along girl.* I made my bow and took my leave, accompanied by two of the sincerest people in the world.

We were no sooner got a little way from the house, than Chloe, turning to my friend, said, *I could have beat you; I had no chance to have spoken one word to Mr. A—, but by being cut out.* And, addressing herself to me, *Well, what do you think of my lovers? I assure you, if I do not capitulate to one, I am afraid of being taken by storm by the other. The 'Squire has produced a long rent-roll of an estate, free from all incumbrances—but himself. The Captain attacks me with all the warmth of a passionate lover, with a bold assurance peculiar to the cockade—presuming to kiss me into a compliance—But I gave him a very handsome slap of the face this morning, telling him to remember, I expected to be treated with more respect; I was yet neither his mistress nor his wife. My mother takes the 'Squire's part, thinking it will be an easy matter to get him created a baronet. The Captain takes his own, upon a belief of more powerful assistance.*

My friend, observing me to redden at the account Chloe gave me of the familiar treatment she met with, said to me, *Make yourself easy—be assured of my friendship*: And, speaking to Chloe,

How did the Captain receive the slap of the face? Not with the greatest composure of mind imaginable, she replied. *He would have been angry;* but I prevented him, by saying, *You know my terms, Sir; I will converse with you upon no other.* He affected a smile, and answered, *They are damned hard ones.*

When we came to the Colonel's, he seemed greatly pleased with his company; and, saluting Chloe, he said, *Miss, you must excuse an old fellow. This young gentleman,* meaning myself, *will excuse me. I kissed his mother—a good many years ago, though she was as pretty as you are—almost.*

They thought it would be proper to return directly back, and, only drinking one glass of wine apiece, took their leave: Chloe, at parting, shaking her hand, and saying to me, *Never doubt me.* They were no sooner gone, than my good friend exclaimed, *A girl of spirit! a fine girl indeed!* And, taking hold of me, *Come, let us go, and finish the bottle to her health. You shall stay here tonight; and once for all, I tell you, come here as often as you think proper, or may find it necessary.* I answered him, I should not have troubled him this time, but Mrs. Worthy had such and such company at her house, and I thought it would be inconvenient to stay there, especially as my temper could ill brook, to bear with indifference, to see the addresses others were at liberty to make to Chloe. Adding, *Sir, as to the offer of using your house with freedom as often as I may think it necessary—as my affairs stand, it is too well situated not to advantage myself of it. Do so, do so,* he replied; *and I will keep a good look-out: Though I do not often write, if anything occurs to me that I think you ought to know, I will set pen to paper.—The 'Squire has a large estate, and is greatly altered for the better, yet he will make but an indifferent husband. He is very obstinate, and given greatly to wine and women. He is no fool, but his sense consists chiefly in holding his tongue. Chloe's cousin, I suppose, has introduced him. The parson is a well meaning man, but he should set a higher value upon the girl than to think of making her happy by marrying her to an estate. As for the Captain, or his father, I know nothing of them. I have seen a young gentleman, with a cockade, two or three times in the grounds, with a gun in his hand; I suppose that is he. He is a likely man—You must expect difficulties—Nothing without difficulties—But you have a friend in the place—That ought to make you easy.*

Thus the old gentleman agreeably went on—When he had done, he sat musing some time; and, my thoughts being likewise employed, I did not offer to interrupt him—when he begun again, *Well, let the worst come to the worst, you can but carry her off. But there is danger in that—It is very hazardous—I will tell you what happened to me, when I was a young gay fellow. I do not love to talk of it, but I am, I think, now in the humour.*

CHAPTER XXI

*The Author's Friend relates
an Account of himself, etc.*

"I am the younger brother of a very good family, and, at my father's death, which happened when I was about nine years of age, I found my fortune was, through his great economy and prudent management, twenty thousand pounds, a great sum for a second child. My brother and I, for there were but two of us, were brought up under the immediate care of one of our guardians. He had an only daughter about my age, a very promising young lady of great wit, vivacity and spirit. As we were educated at home, Miss and I became very intimate; and insensibly, as we grew up, came to love each other sincerely. We were about fifteen when we interchanged our promises of mutual fidelity— Then the revolution happened; and the accounts of so many noblemen and gentlemen being in arms, for the defence of their religious and civil rights, so fired my young mind, that, not being able to obtain my guardian's consent to go, I ran away from him; and, making myself known to a gentleman, who had been acquainted with my father, I was presented to the Prince of Orange, and had a pair of colours given me.

"The Prince being crowned King, and a war with France coming on, I went into Flanders; and I cannot now determine, whether ambition or love excited my courage most to distinguish myself. I kept a correspondence with Miss, 'till, by some means or other, one of my letters was intercepted; and her father, who was no friend to the cause I engaged in thought to take a full revenge on me by having her closely watched, and strictly forbid her from ever thinking of me more.

"I tried various schemes, and used all the means I could, when I was in England upon a recruiting party, to get to see her, or to get a letter conveyed to her, but all in vain. She was in the custody of those who thought as he did, and made it a piece of merit to cross our loves.

"Three years passed away, in which time I had got a company. My brother was of age, and in possession of his estate. He wrote to me to come to him, as the Army was going into winter quarters, and his letter furnished me with an opportunity of sending one to my mistress. I immediately obtained leave to come home for two or three months; and, with all the secrecy I could, took up my residence at a little house, near my guardian's—sending my servant with a letter to my brother, intimating I was very much wounded, and should not be able to be in England 'till the following winter.

"This news, I knew from the intimacy between them would be soon communicated to my guardian, and, as I imagined, put him a little off his guard— So far it succeeded. I had given my man a letter for Miss, and furnished him with an answer, if he should be asked how I could spare him to come into England—But this is not material. He was made welcome by my brother's servants, during the time he was to stay; and my brother, two or three times, sent him with messages to Miss's father's: In one of them he delivered my letter, and in another brought me an answer, That she would be ready at twelve o'clock, such a night, at the garden gate.

"I sent my man back to my brother's, with orders to leave the family, and be with me at such a time, the evening she had appointed. He was punctual, and we went about half an hour before twelve to the appointed place, I with great impatience, every minute expecting her; when we were alarmed with the report of a gun, fired from the house. We waited a little, but soon perceived the family was got up, so I thought it best to go to an inn, about a mile off—and long we had not been here, before the news came, that Mr. G——'s daughter was shot in their own garden."

Here the old gentleman paused a little, to give way to a tenderness this melancholy part of his story occasioned: But, recovering himself, he went on—"The next day, the whole came out. One of Mr. G——'s servants said that he had heard a noise, as if somebody was breaking into the house; and, catching up his gun, which stood by his bedside, went to the window, and thought he heard somebody run down the gravel walk—That he fired at random, it being so dark he could not see. I understood, she fell about fifty yards from the house, the ball going in behind her ear. It was supposed that the noise she made in opening the door next to the garden alarmed the fellow: However, I lost the dear girl forever.

"I returned to Flanders, and my despair made me to perform actions, in endeavouring to seek for death, which promoted me to the rank of a lieutenant colonel—Some years ago, I obtained leave to retire, and I bought this little house and ground, and here it is my purpose to end my days."

This story gave a melancholy turn to the rest of our conversation for the evening, and the next morning I set out again for my aunt's.

I told Corinna I had viewed the enemy, and gave her such an account of their strength, as I was judge of. I repeated to her the Colonel's story; adding, *You see, all are not to be happy in love. It is very true,* she replied; *but none ought to be guilty, they deserve their misfortunes*: However, I observed her to be pleased with my quick return. She asked me what measures I intended to take? I answered, *They must depend upon the motions of the enemy: I had good intelligence among them, but I doubt Lucinda. I wish she proves true; she seems too cool. And now, Corinna, if it will be agreeable to you, I will stay here 'till Mr. Trueman's wedding—I have no relish for books or company*—And indeed that was true.

I found the passion I had so long nursed in my bosom, grew troublesome: Chloe's charms grew too mighty to be gazed at only, and my love began to look for more substantial happiness. I had experienced somewhat of womankind, and I longed for pleasures only Chloe could grant. I grew restless, suffered my wishes to indulge themselves, and was in a constant fever.

Wishing to remain steadfast in my resolve to be true to Chloe, I had for some time absented myself from the carousing parties that met at public houses and other such institutions of low repute. Avoiding the company of jades and w—, I was thus constant in my fidelity. However, the tumult of the young juices which ran high in my fevered loins refused to be stilled. Alas, time and time again I found myself resorting to the dubious satisfactions of the solitary vice.

I awoke often, my hands seeking her dear bosom in the warm bed only to discover that I was alone and in need of the discharge of my passions. Lacking all else, I was impelled to resort to the sole remedy available. My every limb trembling with unslaked desires, I was forced to the inferior gratifications of digitation.

Contrary to my better nature, and to the dictates of my own soul, my fevered hands reached downward to that part which cried out most loudly for relief. My fingers sought the inflamed head of my exercised member. Reluctantly, then ensnared in the heat of this solitary activity, my clutching hands encircled the swelled shaft and began their inevitable rhythms.

I writhed in increasing tempos to match the boiling up of those passions which demanded fulfillment, however meagre. My back chafed the smooth sheets beneath me as I endeavoured to fit my member ever more intimately into that cavity formed by my encircling palm.

My singular thrustings and heavings accelerated a pace with my long-denied yearnings and in a moment of volcanic eruption, the sweet liquors of desire flooded themselves over. My hands felt the first spurts of boiling juice. Then the liquid cooled and upon my palms was the sticky sensation of the honey I had wasted in that vexatious endeavour. And in only a short time those desires which I had tried to quench were returned to torment me with their importunate challenges.

So vain, so unsatisfactory were these nocturnal exercises that I redoubled my vow to have Chloe for my own. I could not bear the thoughts of waiting for the death of a woman not much above forty. I must have Chloe—She had told me she was ready to have me, and I had never moved one step towards it. I upbraided myself with not cultivating more acquaintance—I might have found some young parson who would have risked, for a friend, the tacking of a pair together. Mr. Trueman had promised to give her away: He could mean no otherwise than privately, because he knew, as well as myself, there were no hopes of obtaining the mother's consent.

Thus I reasoned—thus I tormented myself. I suffered my passion to prey upon me, 'till an alteration was visible in my countenance. I grew pale and melancholy—unsatisfied love, eating, like a vulture, my heart. My aunt was frightened, and an apothecary sent for; but, what was the use of medicine? My distemper was beyond the power of physic: However, he found a name for the disorder he was ignorant of, and loaded me with preparations to remove it; but Corinna stood my friend, and they were all thrown away.

I made a resolution to be better—I was ashamed of what I could not help. Corinna knew my passion, and generously pitied it. Instead of feeling a pleasure to see me in pain, she soothed it—she flattered it—she removed all difficulties—she brought Chloe to my arms—she talked continually of Chloe, and sounded no other name but Chloe's in my ears.

This was acting "beyond her sex," indeed! But, by her talking upon a subject so agreeable to me, I was prevented from so intensely thinking upon it. I grew better, and the apothecary had his money and my aunt's thanks—while Corinna had mine.

I determined to take more exercise, and accordingly rode out twice a day. In one of these airings, going through a little village, I met with a fellow collegian. We were glad to see one another; and, while we were talking, and I was inquiring what brought him to this part of the world, and he had just informed me, he was curate there, a man came up to him and told him, he had a writ against him, saying, *Sir, as you are a gentleman, I have come to you without my follower; I would not expose you. How much is it?* I asked. He answered, *The debt and writ will be about twenty pounds.*

CHAPTER XXII

The Author relieves the Curate, etc.

Well, Sir, I said, (upon the Curate's exclaiming, *Twenty pounds! I have not twenty shillings!*) *be not uneasy, I will set you free;* and, addressing myself to the bailiff, *if you will come along with me, I will pay you. How far, Sir?* he asked. I answered, *About three miles, to such a place. Indeed,* he replied, *I cannot dance so far after you; it is out of my way. The gentleman shall be well used at my house, and you may come to him; you will find him safe.*

I was heartily vexed at his insolence; but there was no remedy, and turned about to fetch the money, when luckily a farmer came by, who lived next door to my aunt's. I immediately asked him, if he had any quantity of cash about him. *How much do you want?* he said. *Twenty pounds,* says I. *I have not near so much, but I can have it at that house,* he answered. I told him, I should be greatly obliged to him, and he should have it as soon as we got home: Accordingly we went to the house, which proved to be a public one, as well as a farm; and, upon his asking for the money, it was brought.

I discharged the debt, but could not help telling him, *He had caught no gudgeons today.* The inhumanity of the scoundrel vexed me; to refuse to ride three miles, to give a gentleman his liberty—I could have kicked the dog. I remembered what Chloe's cousin had said, "That men of fortune were the gudgeons women of pleasure baited for," and I looked upon the bailiff in that light. He thought of getting him to his house, to run up a bill, which going with me would prevent: But for once he missed his aim, and got not a six-pence for himself. He knew the farmer too well to put any tricks upon him, and I was so vexed at his ill nature that I never asked him to drink—indeed proceeded to business directly, and called for none 'till he was gone.

I then ordered a dinner, and we were passing away our time very merrily, when I was surprized with the sight of Corinna and our scrub: But I was soon let into the secret, that one of the gossips, who knew the bailiff, and had seen us go into the house together, had trotted away to my aunt's, and told her I was arrested; and the old woman, in great concern for me, had ordered her chaise to be got ready, and scrub drove Miss to the place, with forty pounds in her pocket, to bring me away.

We made ourselves very merry at the news, and I immediately repaid the money the honest farmer had borrowed, and obliged my friend to take the rest, telling Corinna, I would give her money to return to her god-mother.

The farmer took notice of the good nature of my aunt, saying to me, *Sir, your aunt is a worthy gentlewoman in the main; and, was it not for the gang of gossips, who deserve hanging, she would be the best neighbour in the country. But she goes so little abroad that they tell her what they please: She gives credit to them because she is unable to contradict them.* I observed that what he said was very just: *Yes, yes, Sir,* he replied, *you know it to be true; but when this young lady and you are in possession, I hope you will clear the house of such vermin.*

We laughed, and assured him we would. *Come along with us,* I said to the curate: *You may ride my horse, and I will get into the chaise with Miss.* This was agreed to, and very merry we made ourselves at our equipage. The chaise, I will answer for it, had not been oiled from the time it was bought, and the harness was much in the same order. Scrub was a figure of figures—To be very fine, he had flipped on his best coat, which was yellow trimmed with red, over a dirty striped waistcoat. His breeches were leather, and very greasy. A white wig, made out of calves tails, adorned his head, which was covered with a flapped hat, bound round with an old piece of crepe. Our cattle were of different genders: a broken-winded gelding, and a pot-bellied mare—their tails and manes curiously plaited with straw; but they matched well in their colour and marks.

When we got home, which took up a full hour to do, for the old creatures had long forgot to trot, I introduced my friend (the farmer dropping us at his own house) and then I went to fetch the money to give to Corinna to return to her aunt.

When I came into the room, I found the old gentlewoman expressing her gladness I had a friend with me, when the thing happened, asking the gentleman, how much the debt was? He answered, *Twenty pounds; and, had it not been for the generosity of your nephew, Madam, I must have gone to jail. You, Sir, have gone to jail!* She replied: *for what? Why, Madam,* he answered, *I was the person who was arrested, and Mr. A—has been so kind as to pay the debt and all expenses. Good Lord! good Lord! how I am imposed upon,* she said: *Here came Goody Such-a-one, and told me my nephew was in the hands of a bailiff. It frightened me, and I hastened away my god-daughter to fetch him back. But I am glad she was mistaken; the poor soul, I am sure, did it out of pure good nature.*

Corinna returned her the forty pounds, and my friend and I went into a little room to smoke our pipes and drink a bottle, admiring at the ready excuse the old gentle-woman made for her tale-bearer's imposing upon her.

It came into my head that I might make him an instrument of my happiness, as I had been of his deliverance; and I was beginning to sound him out when Corinna came to tell me my aunt wanted to speak with me. *Then pray, Miss,* I said, *give the gentleman your company 'till I return.* When I came into the room, my aunt told me that she was pleased I had done a gentleman a piece of service, but that she thought it was too much for my pocket, and very cordially returned the twenty pounds to me, saying, *I will give the other to Corinna, send her to me; I will let her come back again.* I returned her my thanks, and, returning to my company, said to Corinna, *Go to your godmother—you will have it—it is your turn now.* She came back soon, and, addressing herself to me, *How could you frighten me so? Well, twenty pounds was quickly got; I should like these short trips at the same price every day.*

I was forced to postpone my own business, as it would have been cruel, I thought, in her presence, to enter upon such a subject as marriage to another, and contented myself, with giving myself an invitation to dine with him the next day.

I hope I shall be excused for saying I was of an open, generous disposition, and that my friendship never varied, like many others, according to the good or bad circumstances of those I had once chosen to rank among the number of my friends. This same disposition led me to treat Corinna with the greatest deference; and, to avoid giving her any uneasiness, from suspecting what I was about, I proposed it to her to walk with me. I knew I should find opportunities enough to talk to him, and I was willing she should think I had no secrets but what she knew: This was strictly hypocrisy, but injurious to no one. She readily complied, and we as readily obtained my aunt's consent.

He entertained us very genteelly, and I took the farther liberty to ask him how much he might be indebted in all at the University. He told me he was sure he now did not owe above twenty-four or twenty-five pounds more. *Then pay it,* I said, *by all means; for, when your creditors know you have paid some, they will be at you again.* He answered me that he would, as soon as possible: That he had but thirty pounds a year for the cure, and he would pay as fast as he received. I replied, *Then let me be your creditor, rather than them,* and obliged him to receive the other twenty pounds—and I found an opportunity to ask him about the favour he would do me to marry me to Chloe. He seemed greatly to hesitate, as being taking a step entirely to ruin him. I told him, he had nothing to fear on that head; that Mr. Trueman, whom he well knew, would give her away in the presence of another gentleman, and they would take upon them to say they saw us married, without naming by whom—and I knew nobody would offer to dispute their words; or, if the worst came to the worst, they had fortune sufficient to indemnify him. He then readily said, *I will do it with all my heart. Your hearts are united; it would be pity to separate you.* All these matters being adjusted, we set out about a fortnight after, as if we were going to take a ride for three or four days to view the country.

CHAPTER XXIII

*The Author goes again to Chloe's.
Meets with a remarkable Disappointment.*

We proceeded to the good Colonel's, and I met with my usual frank reception. He seemed to take a good deal of notice of the Curate, and told me, he smelt a rat, as his phrase was, adding, *This love is the devil—You will have her I see—Well, you shall have my assistance. Though she is a great fortune, you seem to have great merit. I think you deserve her—if I had a daughter I would give her to you.*

This encouraged me fairly to confess the whole scheme—*Well, well,* he said, *bring her here, and I will witness to your tie: Your friend shall come to no harm I warrant him.* My heart leaped with joy —my spirits were all in agitation—Fancy was busy, and Chloe, in imagination, was already in my arms. The delicacy of that charming girl was giving way to a passion of a more pleasing kind—I was all rapture and in this joyful frame of mind set out to see my dear Chloe to confer with her on a time and place at which our marriage could transpire.

I was received at the door of the Worthy household by Mrs. Worthy. *Sir,* said she, *I am afraid I must greet you with somewhat unfortunate words. I assume you are come to see Chloe, she is, however, taken ill. The apothecary has visited and recommends rest and the mildest of salts and headache powders; we thus presume her malady not to be of serious nature, but she is easily fatigued.*

I will not stay overlong, I said, understanding this last to be aimed for my benefit. I was, however, much alarmed by this news, though somewhat calmed by the apothecary's prescribed treatment.

I expressed to Mrs. Worthy my anxiety respecting the poor dear girl but in terms designed to conceal the depth of my true sentiments.

I am sure a visit from you would do much to raise her spirits, said Mrs. Worthy graciously. I followed her to the bed-chamber where Chloe was a-bed, pale but lovely.

I thought a visit from Mr. A—would not displease you, said Mrs. Worthy.

Indeed it would not, replied Chloe politely. Her mother withdrew, leaving us in silence regarding one another for many moments.

Finally, seating myself at her bedside, I exclaimed, *My poor dear angel! What has happened?"*

I fear I am much worn down by the pressures exerted in this household, she replied, *by all parties —save, of course, your kind friend Mr. Trueman. It is a continual thing and grows in intensity with each new day.* She paused, ... *and I do so long to be with you.*

I was so distressed, yet so impassioned, by this pronouncement that I could no longer wait to give her my news.

My love, I whispered, all is arranged for our wedding. I have the Curate's promise to preside, and the good Colonel will gladly serve as witness where and whenever we may choose. I see from your state you are in no position to oblige me with a firm decision; but I cannot tell you how anxious I am that you be truly mine, and how distraught I am over the present circumstance.

Chloe smiled, the fresh colour of her cheeks even seeming to have heightened since my first view of her but half an hour before.

It grieves me, I went on, *to leave you here a moment longer, surrounded as you are by those at odds with our own desires.*

I cannot compare vexation to mine, and our disorders are alike; but Lucinda was not so kind to me, nor has she once mentioned your name to me since her brother has begun his visits: But my letter has the full account in it. I am greatly obliged to Corinna. I own I love you, and my love increases every day—Opposition adds to it; and I am happy to be a little free from continual solicitation. As my mamma courts for the 'Squire, my illness has stopped her saying anything lately. He is rambling somewhere, and the Captain is gone, for two or three months, to the Regiment, and, thank my stars, will not be at his sister's wedding. Lucinda's father, I believe, will carry my mamma. I answered, *I cannot see any advantage in that to us. But why do we wait? Why do we not take the present opportunity and be gone?*

And where, says she, *will you carry me to?*

Fool that I was, I had never thought of that. I had provided no secure and secret retreat for my treasure. She saw my surprize, and that I was unprepared to answer her question, and kindly said, *We must have a little patience; though if I were able to go with you, I would not hesitate a moment—but trust all to fortune. We shall be here again early in the spring, and, if I am not free from both my lovers, I will follow you where you please. And if, Madam, you are,* I asked, gravely, *what then?—Why then,* says she, *I believe, I shall do so too.*

I conjured her to take care of her health; and, taking leave of her, returned to my friends to dinner. I told them I was about to bring her off, and why she refused. The Colonel said, *These young fellows are so hot, they never give themselves time to think; the girl has more sense then ten of you: However, I have a place for you in my eye—if it comes to running away. I will say nothing, nor shall anyone know it but yourself, and then nobody can tell.*

After dinner we set out for home once more, my friend expressing himself greatly pleased with the frank open temper of the old gentleman. When I came to my aunt's, I had the following letters delivered to me, from Mr. Trueman and Chloe.

"*My good friend,*

I should think myself greatly deficient in the friendship I profess to you, if I did not give you an account of what is doing here. Your Chloe is strongly besieged, but she defends herself bravely: However they have teased her so much, that what between her love for you, and their solicitations for another, she is greatly altered. Her mother and the cousin are for the 'Squire: The cousin preaches up obedience, and Chloe answers him with inclination. She is ill, but I hope will get over it. Lucinda's brother too is a lover, and, I am sorry to say, Lucinda is not so earnest for you as she used to be: However, I have begged of her, out of regard to me, not to offer to uncover anything she knows between you. Lucinda's father will certainly carry Chloe's mamma. He has endeavoured to get me to solicit for his son, assuring me, if he succeeded, he should think himself obliged to make Lucinda an handsome fortune. I answered him that I asked no fortune with his daughter, but was obliged to him for his consent. As to endeavouring to persuade Chloe, I knew she was not insensible of merit, but that I had no notion of compelling inclinations: That I should not have applied to him, had I not had Lucinda's permission. He replied he was an utter enemy to compulsion, but it was natural for him to wish to see his son so well settled. This is all material. I go for London tomorrow, and expect you, out of friendship to me, to be at my wedding. I shall be at Lucinda's father's, 'till

I have taken a ready furnished house. Come to town soon.

I am yours sincerely,

John Trueman."

"SIR,

I am in a very unfit temper of mind to write, but you claim a right to know what happens to me. I am so strongly pressed by my mother and my cousin to accept of the 'Squire for an husband, that I am quite another thing. I neither eat nor sleep. My thoughts are all upon you, while they are constantly urging me to another: This preys on me so, that I am worth no one's having. The Captain treats me now with great complaisance; but Lucinda, instead of affording me any comfort, is continually praising her brother, and recommending to me to be dutiful. I ask her if she would have me faithless? She says she never would have engaged farther with anyone, than as it should have been agreeable to her father's consent. I replied, at that rate she might coquet it with half the young fellows in town, and break off very fairly, whenever he thought proper. Then she is so much taken up with the thoughts of her approaching finery, that I am afraid her little heart is full of a great deal of pride.

"However, they shall never carry their point. I have made a resolution to starve myself by degrees, and am already so ill that the 'Squire, finding he is not likely to have me soon, has set out upon another tour somewhere, with two of his companions. The Captain is going to his Regiment, and tomorrow we shall have a clear house. I wish you would come and see me—Do if you can. If I die, you may assure yourself, I die for you.

Chloe."

This letter would have given me great uneasiness, had it come before I set out to see her, but now I knew she was out of all danger. I made sure of the Curate against another time, and he promised me to keep everything secret. I had no doubt of that, as he was an enemy to gossiping and mischief-making.

We were constantly together 'till the time drew on that I had proposed to go to London. I had a double pleasure in going to the wedding; obliging my friend, and the full hope of seeing Chloe. I told Corinna the marriage of Mr. Trueman was approaching. She replied, *And your own, I suppose. May you be happy.* I assured her mine, if it ever was to be, was a great way off, and showed her the letter I had from Chloe. She seemed to be really affected with the melancholy account she gave of her situation, saying, *I would not have her die.*

She pleased me so much with these marks of her good nature, that I went and bought a gold watch, and insisted upon her accepting it, and wearing it was a mark of my esteem. This my aunt took extremely well, imagining her intended scheme would certainly take place; and when I acquainted her that I was going to my friend's wedding, she answered, *I hope it will not be long before you can return the compliment, and invite him to yours.*

CHAPTER XXIV

The Author goes to London.

I set out, very early in the morning; and, as soon as I quitted my horse, went, booted as I was, to Lucinda's father's. They had just sat down to dinner—only themselves: Mr. Trueman, the father, and Lucinda. My friend expressed great pleasure at my having come. I answered, *I was happy in seeing him so near being so.* Miss behaved with great ceremonious civility. Mr. Trueman observing it, said, *My dear, this gentleman is no stranger to us;* and, speaking to me, *I expect you to make this your home. I do not mean to confine you, but here you will always be welcome*—The father said the same.

Upon my inquiring how Mrs. and Miss Worthy did? Lucinda replied, maliciously enough, *Chloe has been very ill; but I suppose you know they came to town last night. They sent to me this morning, but I was going out to buy some things, and have not seen them—I propose to go this afternoon.* I assured her I did not know it; that I was sorry for Miss's illness, and would do myself the honour to inquire after her health. She answered, *I am surprised at that.* My friend looked grave and said, *We will, if you please, go with you. Then, I am sure,* says she, *we shall carry agreeable company with us.*

Lucinda's father desired his compliments, but, as he was obliged to meet a gentleman about business, he would defer his visit 'till morning—Accordingly we three set out.

Mrs. Worthy, upon our coming in, in a very affable manner, said, *This is as it should be—I am glad we are all met together once more.* Chloe said much the same; but, I took notice the young ladies carried it to one another as if they expected soon to fall out. The first opportunity I had to speak to Chloe, I expressed my pleasure in seeing her so well recovered, and begged of her to carry it to Lucinda with her usual freedom. She answered, *I will, if I can; but I am sure she will prove a snake in the grass.* We could say no more then, for Lucinda seemed to take pains to hinder, and a secret pleasure in preventing our talking together.

Mr. Trueman appeared to be very uneasy, and proposed to me to go to the coffee-house, saying to Mrs. Worthy, *Madam, I only called now to pay my respects to you, and to bid you welcome to town; I will take another time for a longer visit*—And away we went, leaving Lucinda to pass the evening there.

Chloe's mother, at our going, was pleased to say to me, *Sir, I know the difference there is between you and your father, and I desire you to make free with my table.* Lucinda answered for me, *I will engage for Mr. A—.* There was nothing in her expressions to give umbrage; but the manner of speaking them convinced me that she was endeavouring to raise a jealousy of me.

Instead of going to the coffee house, my friend altered his mind, and we went to a neighbouring tavern, and there Mr. Trueman gave me fresh assurances of serving me, saying, *I cannot bear the thoughts of sacrificing two friends, to aggrandize a stranger; for such my brother-in-law, as is to be, is, when compared to Chloe and yourself. If one of you must have her, exclusive of my friendship for you, I should determine in favour of her inclinations. I imagine, however sanguine her mother is now in the interest of the 'Squire, my father-in-law will bring her over to his son's; for I can tell you,* entre nous, *they have settled the grand point between them, and you will be at two weddings, instead of one: But I insist upon it, you keep this a secret from Chloe.* I thanked him, and answered, *Sir, I never *made the least doubt of your friendship, if I had occasion to use it*—And told him the whole affair, of my having engaged an acquaintance of ours to marry me to Chloe privately, and the disappointment I met with. He answered, *Nothing could have been more unlucky: But she was very ill, and her spirits could not bear fatigue*—Adding, *Our friend shall know I approve his conduct; in serving you, he shall find he serves me.*

I inquired when his marriage was to be, and he told me in about a fortnight: *You shall know the particular day, for I shall expect you at it.* I replied, *I came to town on purpose, but I am afraid it will not be so agreeable to Lucinda; she treats me too ceremoniously, and, rather than give her the least umbrage, I should choose to stay away.* No, no, he answered, *I again insist upon your being there—There will be Chloe. I love Lucinda sincerely, but I will not suffer her to make a fool of me.*

We parted and I went to my inn. The next morning my tailor and I were in deep consultation about equipping me to make a proper, decent appearance. That important point being settled, I proceeded to Chloe's, and found her just going to take a walk, and had her mother's permission to wait on her; who said, *As Mr. A—is with you, you will have no occasion for a servant.*

We were very well pleased to go without one—I saw she had been crying, and asked her what had occasioned it? She said, *The old affair—my mamma has acquainted me, in a very peremptory manner, that she will be obeyed—that as I am very well now, she expects me to receive the 'Squire upon his return, as a person I approve of for an husband. This occasioned a little bickering; she was positive, and I cried.*

I told her, I thought it would be the best method she could pursue to receive the 'Squire civilly, without giving him any particular encouragement; that, by so doing, she would get time, and might easily protract the courtship 'till they went into the country, when she might assure herself, I would be ready to prevent her being compelled, if she would take care not to give me another impediment, by illness. She promised to be guided by me, and we fell into discourse concerning the preparations for the ensuing wedding. *I am to be very fine,* she said. *You will see me dressed—You never saw me dressed—Are you to be fine too, to honour your friend?* I answered, *No, Miss; I have pitched upon a mouse-coloured cloth, and have ordered my tailor to make me a frock, waistcoat and breeches, out of the piece, only ornamenting it with a narrow silver lace. Grave and genteel!* she replied. *Oh! but Lucinda and I tiffed a little last night. She stayed to supper with us, and my mamma very liberally bestowed commendations upon her, for her ready compliance in everything with her papa's desires: Adding, "How happy might Chloe be, if she would pay the same obedience to me?" I answered, "I should be happy to have my inclinations and duty go together." Lucinda replied that she thought that mighty easy; if people would not give way to inclinations 'till they were sure they would correspond with their duty. She thought parents had an unlimited power; and, however she loved a man, she could part with him, if her papa commanded her. "Your love then," I said, "Miss, is very indifferent." "No, no," answered my mamma, "her discretion is very great." "Indeed, Miss," Lucinda added, "I fixed my love upon such an object, that I was in no fear of my papa's disapprobation—I was sure the man I loved could maintain me." Thus she proceeded, with a great many innuendos: I loved somebody, and somebody loved me. However, my mamma took no notice of them, as it happened; and, about twelve, she swung home in a chair—so happy!—so self-contented! She has a great many good qualifications, but I wish Mr. Trueman does not find she overrates them.*

I took my leave of Chloe at her own door, being somehow disposed to be alone. I confess her company grew painful—My passion was too violent to be restrained. I longed to possess the darling creature. To remove lovingly the garments that hid her charms from my probing eyes was my burning desire. To kiss again those adorable breasts: to feel the nipples stiffen with the energies of sweet excitement; to rub my tongue against that fair hardness and to bite with my lover's teeth that erect aureole of aroused passion.

I longed to feel her small hands round my strong member, grown to ever greater dimension by the ferocity of my passions. My darling would chafe that mountainous tower of my desire for her and run her moist tongue along its length and around its overswollen head. Then I in my turn would pay homage with my mouth to that very temple of delights hidden beneath the torrent of golden curls that sprang in triangular conformation just beneath her silken belly. I would take the throbbing mark of her sex, white in the surrounding vermilion flesh, between my teeth and thus rouse my Chloe to an ecstasy never before felt on earth.

Then, fitting my sword to her adorable sheath, we would move as one toward the summit of our pleasure. I would endeavour to impale her still further and she would strain her thighs to permit my probing engine yet greater access to the deepest entrance of her precious orifice. Moving in unison, the sounds of the creaking bed in harmony with our excited writhings, we would mingle our love juices and come away in perfect satisfaction the one with the other.

My thoughts went on in this wise and it was with some effort that I diverted them to less tormenting avenues. I dined by myself, and, in the evening, went to the play.

At dinner time I waited again upon my friend. We were soon left alone, for Lucinda had a dozen shops to fly to that afternoon; and her father was going to the lawyer to get the deeds of settlement finished. Mr. Trueman said, he had heard something about a little quarrel between the girls. I gave him Chloe's account of it, and he expressed himself to be displeased with Lucinda. *I will speak to her again,* says he, *and they shall make it up.* He then showed me the jewels he had bought to present his wife with. They were very curious; and, giving me a diamond ring, *This,* he said, *you must present to Chloe. If she is asked any questions, let her say it was a present from me.*

While we were thus employed, Chloe came in to visit Lucinda, and I had a very fair opportunity to put the ring upon her finger, begging her often to look at it, and think of me. She said she did that already, and wanted no remembrance; but, as it came from me, she would wear it.

We passed our time very sociably, 'till Lucinda returned; and my friend having talked a little in private with her, she came to Chloe—and, kissing her, said, *My dear, I beg your pardon; let us be friends.* Thus I passed my time between the two families, 'till the wedding.

CHAPTER XXV

*Lucinda's Marriage.
The Author returns into the Country.*

At length the wished-for morning came; and, at ten o'clock, the time appointed, I went to Lucinda's father's. My friend was dressed extremely gay, and his countenance fully expressed his happiness. In a little time Chloe's mother, herself, and Lucinda came into the room. Lucinda behaved with a very decent composedness. Chloe looked very gay, and was as fine as clothes could make her. Her mother and Lucinda's father were very richly dressed, but grave. Inclination divided us into couples, and Chloe fell to my share. *I can tell you news*, says she. I answered, *Your mother is to be married. I am very glad of it*, she replied; *I hope Mr. Trueman will be able to rid me of the 'Squire—His father-in-law will surely oblige him so far. Yes, my dear angel, I dare say he will*, I answered—*to make room for his son.*

We went to church, and I observed Chloe to look extremely dull—It immediately occurred to her thoughts, that there would now be a strong interest formed to make the Captain's fortune, at the expense of her happiness.

After the ceremony was over, we went to Chloe's Mother's; that being the largest house, it had been agreed the nuptials should be kept there. Chloe took the first opportunity to tell me that my last words to her had so alarmed her, she should be but very indifferent company: Adding, *I see the whole scheme now. Pull up your spirits*, I said, *they cannot break with the 'Squire directly—They will want you to do that for them; and, if you seem not to express any great dislike, but appear indifferent, you will gain time, and put them to the necessity of finding means to disapprove of what your mother has already so warmly approved of. Well then,* she answered, *all things may not be so bad as they appear. But I know the worst—they shall not fret me into another illness, I assure you.*

With this resolution she cleared up her countenance, and was very pleasant company. The clergyman who had performed the ceremony dined with us, and was of great service in keeping the conversation from being any way particular. I took my leave about eleven o'clock at night, calling every day, for about a week, upon them—and then I set out for the country again. But the evening before I went out of town, when I came to my inn, I found a letter from my friend to me. I was surprised, as I had just parted with him, and could not imagine what he had to write that he could not speak—and, in great uneasiness, opened his letter, and read—

"My good Friend,

I was resolved to have no denial, so have taken this method to convey to you some part of the acknowledgment I owe to your friendship. I am no stranger to your circumstances—The dependence upon old women is very precarious. Accept the enclosed, and let me recommend it to you not to break in upon your two thousand pounds—That will be a sure friend upon any emergency. Command me at your pleasure—You may depend upon my friendship to serve you to the utmost with Chloe. Wishing you a good journey,

I am yours sincerely,

John Trueman."

Upon examining into the contents of the enclosed, I found five bank-notes, of one hundred pounds each, and one of twenty-five pounds, to which was pinned a small direction, *For your Friend the Rev. Mr.—.* This was a real mark of friendship, and a great proof of the generosity of his temper.

When I came to my aunt's, I had work enough upon my hands to give an account of the wedding, the fine clothing, the coach, the horses, the jewels, etc. etc. etc. In the morning I took Corinna in my hand, and we walked over to see my friend the curate. As we were going along she told me, that although it was the general opinion of the country we should make a match, and which she had never contradicted that it might not prejudice my interest with her god-mother, yet my friend had offered to make love to her, and had intimated that he knew my engagement to another. So, thought I, more perplexities—I shall be in a difficult situation. I knew I was the most unfit person in the world to be acquainted with a secret of this sort. I had been too much interested; it was too nice a point for me to speak to. I should have been very well pleased to have had a courtship gone on unknown to me; but now I became a party concerned, and was unable to give an answer. She observed my uneasiness, and said to me, *Give yourself no trouble about me—I will never marry—I can never expect to have you, and I will have no other—I will manage so, as not to affront him.*

When we came to the curate's, he showed me a letter from my friend to him, wherein he had assured him, that in serving me, he should think himself served; and that he might depend upon the first living that fell in his gift; and, to convince him he promised no more than he intended to perform, he had sent him a note for twenty-five pounds. *I am extremely glad of it,* I said; *I know him to be a gentleman of his word, and I am proud to be the bearer of the fellow to it.*

He took an opportunity to mention to me his regard for Corinna, and desired my interest to promote his suit. I asked him if he had spoken to her. He answered, *Yes; but she received me very coldly. Well, well, I replied, we will see what is to be done—Time and perseverance may do much.* This satisfied him, and he behaved so respectfully to her, that I fifty times repented my intimacy with her.

As we were returning home, Corinna said, *I believe I can guess at your private conversation. You are to be his advocate—How happy will you be to be rid of me?* I ingenuously confessed he had spoken to me concerning her, and acquainted her with my answer: Adding, *As to parting with you, I solemnly declare I wish I could make you mine*—and then told her how affairs were between Chloe and me, saying, *I must provide against the worst, and for that purpose I will make another visit to the good old Colonel's.*

When we came home, we were surprized to find two strange gentlewomen with my aunt, a mother and daughter, but soon learned that my aunt and the mother had formerly been very intimate, and that the visit was purely out of regard to old friendship. The mother was a plain, good sort of a person—the daughter might be called a very agreeable, black, pretty woman. She was about twenty-three, a widow, and had become so within a month after marriage. She seemed of a very amorous disposition, and, presuming upon the privilege of having been married, was not over delicate in the manner of expressing herself. She had her own fortune, about five thousand pounds, and a jointure of two hundred pounds a year.

My aunt was very well pleased seemingly at seeing them—The young one she had, indeed, never seen before, and I found we should have their company for a month or two. The old people were so taken up with repeating old stories, and answering one another's questions about such-a-one, and such-a-one, that we three had our entire liberty to go where, and do what we pleased. Corinna was glad to be more at leisure, and eased of being continually with her god-mother; and, being fully convinced of my sincere passion for Chloe, took no notice of the little familiar freedoms which often passed between the widow and me. The widow, on the other hand, was no stranger to the fact I was designed for Corinna by my aunt; but whether to assert the power of her charms, or from a real desire of renewing pleasures she had only tasted, grew very particular to me, and would scarce ever suffer me to be alone, or go anywhere without her.

We were continually visiting my friend, and he was glad to catch every opportunity of speaking to Corinna, who, being determined never to marry, one day gave him his final answer—Letting him know that her heart was engaged, and she would never give her hand unless her inclinations went with it. He knew the widow's circumstances, and made himself easy with the denial, resolving to make his addresses to her, after a little more acquaintance. This latter part I was a stranger to—the event only proving it—But the time came that I proposed to make my visit, as I before-mentioned; and I was quickened to do it by the following letter from Lucinda's husband.

"*My good Friend,*

Chloe's conduct puzzles the whole family, except myself—She manages well. The 'Squire has renewed his visits, and she receives them so composedly, that my father-in-law and my Lucinda think she is willing to have him. This gives them great uneasiness. Lucinda now tells me she could not have thought it of Chloe, that she would prove faithless. I laugh, and answer her, *She is dutiful.* Chloe has desired me not to take it ill, but she cannot consent to let Lucinda into the motive of her present conduct. The old lady too seems disconcerted, and Chloe is at present the only contented person in their family. The Captain is sent for to town, and I would have you be prepared against all events. Excuse compliments.

I am yours sincerely,

John Trueman."

Accordingly, pretending I was obliged to go to Oxford, acquainting only Corinna with the truth, I set out. When I came to the Colonel's, he expressed great satisfaction, saying, *I thought I had hinted enough to you last time to have brought you here sooner. How does the young lady? Is it off?* I told him the whole, and that my present visit was to be prepared against all events. *Well, well,* he answered, *I have got a place for you—an haunted house; but you must lie the closer, that's all. And pray,* say I, *what sort of a spirit troubles it? An imaginary one,* he replied. *We will go tomorrow and see the place—You will approve of it, I am sure.*

Accordingly the next morning, after a walk of about three miles, we came to a solitary house by the side of a wood. It seemed to have been built at twice; one part appeared to be inhabited, the other not, there being pieces of wood nailed in place of glass.

When we went in, an elderly man said, *Colonel, I am very glad to see you. Thank you Serjeant,* he replied. *I have brought the young gentleman I spoke to you about, to view the house.* Which, when I had seen, I thought no place could be so proper. The uninhabited part consisted of an handsome parlour, with a bed-chamber over it and a garret. There was a large garden walled in; the windows in front, as I observed, were nailed up. *These must stand as they are,* I said; *we must have no outward alterations.*

We agreed for everything; and, upon my mentioning getting a maid, *No, no, there will be no occasion,* he said, *my old woman will do best.* I was pleased to observe a good stock of poultry about; *These, my good Friend,* say I, *must be kept up; they will be of great service. But how can we furnish this apartment, without giving suspicion of its being inhabited?* This took us up some consideration, and we thought ourselves all aground. But the Serjeant at last fetched us out of that difficulty, saying, *There are things often left here for such a gentleman, which came from London by such a wagon. I pay for them, and carry them to him. Now you may order anything, and have it directed to be left here, and I will take care to put all things to rights.*

I gave my host some money, and told him that whatever was sent to his house should be his own at last. As we returned back, I asked the Colonel the history of the ghost. *Why,* he replied, *that little place belonged to a tradesman in London. He was born in that house, and, being very successful in business, retained a great affection for the place of his nativity. When he retired from town, he built that part you are to have for himself, and let a man and his wife live in the other rent-free, for giving him what attendance he might want. As he kept himself very close, and was reputed rich, the man villainously murdered him; and the country-people saw so many strange things afterwards, and reported so many frightful stories, that nobody would live in it. At last this man, who was my Serjeant and had saved some money, and got a wife with more, took the house, the person who was landlord being very glad to let him have it for a trifle. He lives there very comfortably, and now and then pays me a visit. I look upon him as a valuable neighbour; and, having often been a witness of his bravery, we dine and drink our bottle together. I asked him if he ever heard or saw anything in his house? He said, He never did; but if the old gentleman had hid any money, he should be glad if he would come and tell him where. In one of his visits to me I mentioned you to him, thinking it would be a proper place for you. He readily agreed to it—I will engage for his honour; and, I am sure, if you are forced to carry the young lady off, if they offer five thousand pounds for her, he will never discover you—He is, I assure you, too gallant an old fellow.*

My good friend was a great enemy to procrastination, and, as soon as he had dined, wrote to an upholsterer to send down, by such a carriage, complete furniture for a bed-chamber.

About ten days after the old Serjeant came, and acquainted us one room was fit to receive a duchess. *Well,* answered the old gentleman, *and so shall the other.*

We dined together, and they fought their battles over again, to my very great entertainment, who was always pleased to hear accounts of our military transactions from the mouths of the parties concerned, when they were men of veracity.

In a short time we learned the whole was complete, and my friend proposed our going to spend a day there. Indeed I was surprized to see how much e erything was in order, and I found a cellar stored to stand a siege. I begged to know the expenses, but was answered, *It is time enough, let us see how matters go first; expenses come fast enough.* I stayed here about two months, and then proceeded round by London home.

CHAPTER XXVI

*The author goes to London—To his Aunt's.
His Surprize, when he came to his Aunt's.*

Mr. Trueman was glad to see me: He seemed greatly pleased, and I soon was informed Lucinda was with child. *I must*, my friend said, *carry her into the country; she must lie-in in our old-fashioned state-bed, as the women have done in our family for some centuries. We have not had an heir born out of the mansion-house for ages.*

Lucinda inquired if I had seen Chloe? I answered, *No. I am sorry for you*, she said; *I am afraid you will lose her, the 'Squire and she are always together, though I believe her mamma is not so fond of the match as she was; and I assure you, my papa is greatly against it, and if he can will prevent it. How will you bear the loss of her?* I replied, *Madam, I have the same affection for Chloe I ever had—I retain the same passion for her, but I cannot expect her to sacrifice everything to me— Though to lose her, I am sure, would go near to cost me my life. Well*, says she, *I do not know how it is, but she is greatly altered—She never mentions your name now. I really believe you are indifferent to her. Then, Madam,* I said, *I had better be without her, for indifference in a wife would never suit my temper. I am going out to take the air*, says she, *and if you please I will call upon her. I will set you down, and take you up again to come to dinner with us. Do so, do so,* my friend said; *and I will go and write my letters now, that we may have the afternoon to ourselves.*

Lucinda stopped at her father's but was told by the servant only Miss was at home: When, speaking to me, *I will not interrupt you; I will leave you here, and call when I come back.*

146

I found Chloe reading, and she seemed greatly surprized to see me. *How do you do! how do you do!* she said: *I am glad to see you!* and, getting up, came into the middle of the room to meet me. *My dear Chloe,* I said, catching her in my arms, *you look charming; I am come to wish you joy. I have heard how indifferent I am to you, but I was willing to be satisfied of the truth from your own mouth.* Oh, she answered, *Lucinda has told you—I believe she had rather you should have me than the 'Squire. I am as happy as I can wish—I have now all the sport to myself—Your friend only is in my design, and I know he has informed you how indifferent you are to me. I am grown the veriest hypocrite—I almost suspect my love for you to be hypocrisy*—and inclining towards me, permitted me to kiss her.

At the meeting of our lips, the passions I had for so long suppressed within me were aroused in an instant.

Oh, my darling Chloe, I whispered, kissing her more fiercely than before, *how long have I awaited a taste of the sweet nectar of your lips.*

My own ardour kindled my darling's passions and her pointed tongue hesitantly found its way through my open lips. I fair swooned with ecstasy. Still holding her in my arms I bent my head and kissed the tender skin along the column of her neck where the great vein throbbed bluish beneath the transparent skin. I sucked deeply her fragile flesh. Ambrosia could not have tasted more sweetly. When I removed my lips I saw that I had raised fair Chloe's blood to the surface of the skin leaving on her throat a mark of my desire sure to last three days.

In quest of still more exquisite pleasures my hands roamed over my darling's body until they came to rest upon her ripe entrancing breasts. I gently disengaged them from the confines of her stays and devoted myself to their sweet-featured enjoyments. Small, but finely fleshed without any particle of excess plumpness they were at once so round, so tightly drawn and firm that they stood pertly in no need of any stay. Their small, delicate nipples, just beginning to harden in response to the passions our exercises were eliciting in Chloe's ardent but yet innocent soul, were of a golden topaz color that far surpassed the memories I had so oft delighted in in the solitary confines of my bachelor bed. Bending to kiss them, first the one and then the other, my shy Chloe inflamed at last by a desire that could no longer be contained, let her hands wander likewise all over my person in search of enjoyment.

How I thrilled to the hot touch of her gentle hands. How I longed for us to be alone; to be able to pursue our quest for pleasure in each other's yearning bodies in the privacy and enveloping warmth of the marital bed.

Making bold in response to Chloe's own passions I lifted her skirts and pressed my way under the lace-edged petticoats. I ran my finger up her firm thighs, revelling in the tender skin that overlaid the inner thigh of my darling girl.

She trembled; she shook as if stirred by a mighty tempest. But I did not stop, having but begun to reach the object of my long quest.

My stealing fingers felt the wiry curls of her delightful moss; that sweet moss that led the way to the most ecstatic delights. I twigged the downy curls between my fingers, causing my Chloe to shake yet again with an excess of pleasure. I combed that downy nest back and forth, round and round in an avid passion to please both my own desires and to serve the enjoyments of my beloved Chloe.

As I pressed on seeking the rigid clit that I knew would be hidden in the forward part of her virgin cleft, I felt her arms tighten round me with alarm.

What is it, my darling? I asked, refraining for the moment from the completion of the exploration my hot hands were carrying out hidden beneath the curtain of her skirts.

Oh, we mustn't, the frightened girl pleaded.

Reluctantly my hands paused in their delightful occupation; but I knew that I must heed my darling's plea else risk being denied forever the delights I had so long resolved to possess.

Removing my fingers from her exquisite Venus temple, I acceded to my love's wishes.

Gathering my scattered wits about me, I then told her the reason of my coming to town was to acquaint her that everything was ready for her reception. I described the place to her; and how, through the care and by the order of my good old friend the Colonel, it was already elegantly furnished—But, as I imagined, if she was obliged to take the desperate resolution to run away, she would not be able to bring any things with her, I should be glad to know her pleasure, that she might suffer no inconvenience it was in my power to prevent. To this she answered, *Give me a direction, I will take care of all those things before we leave town; and assure yourself, that before I will be forced to be another's there is no resolution so desperate I will not attempt to take—My love will give me courage—and now I leave you to judge how indifferent you are to me.*

She then informed me how fond her father-in-law and mamma were of each other—*They are so loving a couple,* she said, *my mamma can deny him nothing. She has already bought her son-in-law a company—He is now a Captain in earnest—He just left me when you came in. He courts me with all the assurance of success; and, I believe, thinks my consent unnecessary. The 'Squire, indeed, treats me with more humanity; he comes to visit me every day, but never troubles me with his passion. He has not spoke an hundred words to me since we were acquainted. His acres are to supply the deficiency of his words, and the largeness of my settlement is to make amends for his want of sense. They have their spies upon him, and every now and then I am entertained with an account of his mad pranks, in some loose house or another: But however mad he may be in a bagnio, he is tame enough here. He is so little used to the company of women of character that, for fear of offending, he says nothing. The most words I ever heard at one time come out of his mouth were in praise of a fox-hound he brought with him. When they tell me of his loose behaviour, I express no resentment. My father-in-law indeed is a subtle gentleman—He does not think I like the 'Squire; and, I am sure, believes I do like someone but whom he cannot find out. Nobody comes after me, and the notion of your Corinna takes off all suspicion from you.*

She was thus entertaining me, when Lucinda's coach stopped, and up she came. *So! so! I find you together*, she said. *Well, Sir, how do you find Chloe now?* Chloe answered, *He says he has heard of my indifference—I have a fine time between love and duty! I tell him how people ought not to mind what silly young girls say before they are at years of discretion. He pretends to be constant, and I believe would willingly have me so.* The coming in of her mother prevented more; and Lucinda saying, *We shall make Mr. Trueman stay dinner*, we departed.

When we were in her coach, she said, *I told you so; who could have thought it! Could you have thought it! With what great indifference she behaved! Did you quarrel?* I answered, No, Madam; I love Chloe too well to dispute her pleasure. I was all attention, and heard all she said with great patience.

By this time we were got to my friend's; and in a little time after we had dined, Lucinda went to dress, having a dozen or two of visits to make that evening, leaving her husband and me to ourselves. We were greatly pleased with Chloe's artful conduct—*The charming hypocrite! I said. I could never have believed her capable of playing a part so different from her natural temper so well. She does it admirably well.* Mr. Trueman answered, *I cannot give her conduct so harsh a name as hypocrisy. She deceives no one. She encourages neither of her lovers; one, by the paternal authority, she must give her company to; the other is permitted to make his addresses, and she hears him. He expects she will be ready to receive him, when the lawyers are agreed; and, I dare say, regards her no more than as a pretty girl, who may bring an heir to his estate. He must have a wife; she is handsome, and a great fortune. The Captain may value her a great deal; but, I dare say, values her estate more. His father is a worldly man—My courting his daughter brought him acquainted with Chloe's mother. He has gained her, and will endeavour all he can to carry Chloe for his son; and I am more afraid of her being compelled to this match, than the other. He has told me he is sure Chloe's affections are settled upon someone, and asked me if I knew the young lady you were to have? I answered him, I had seen her; she was very pretty, and your aunt's fortune was to be divided between you: That the old gentlewoman's heart was set upon the match, and I could not imagine you could do better, as your dependance was upon her. He said it was only a surmise, grounded upon Chloe's quick recovery—Her mother has observed she recovered very speedily after you had been there. "He is," he added,* a very fine gentleman, but I must not suffer her inclinations to bestow her fortune where she pleases; in duty she ought to oblige her mother." *I replied I thought she showed a great deal of duty in receiving the addresses of the 'Squire. "Oh!" he answered, "that shall be broken off." This,* said my friend, *I had this morning; I will tell Chloe the first time I see her.*

Thus we passed our time 'till I thought it would be proper to go to my inn—*No, no,* he said, *I have ordered a bed—This house is my own—My servant shall fetch your horse to my stables in the morning. Whenever I am in town, I expect you to make this your home.* I gave him a large and full description of the retreat I had prepared for Chloe, if matters were pushed to extremity. *Your description,* says he, *convinces me it has been expensive. I commend you for showing her all the respect due to her merit, and the life she has been bred in—She has been used to seeing everything elegant. What might it cost you?* I answered him that I knew not; that my good friend the Colonel had taken the whole management of it upon himself, and given directions for everything. But he would not tell me the cost, and repeated his words. Mr. Trueman replied, *I love that good-natured man: But it is so almost with all those gentlemen who are truly brave—Generosity generally attends true courage. He seems to like you extremely; and, I dare say, old as he is, would draw his sword in the cause of Chloe.*

Thus we passed the evening 'till Lucinda's return; and then we had a full account of where she had been, of those she had seen, and those she had not—We supped, and then retired.

The next day, after breakfast, I told my friend I would take the mornings to make a collection of books; as my good friend had furnished the cellar plentifully, I would furnish out somewhat for the amusement of the mind. He obligingly said, *I will accompany you; for I know no way of spending time better than going from one collection of books to another—One picks up something here and there worth fetching.*

Thus we passed our mornings, 'till I had got as many books as I thought necessary, and I sent them away. The particular regard Mr. Trueman expressed for me, gave me all the opportunities I could desire of seeing Chloe. Lucinda grew suspicious that she was left out of some secret, but she could not tell what: However, I thought it proper to return into the country; and, being assured of Chloe's resolution and Mr. Trueman's friendship, after an absence of little more than two months, I came once more to my aunt's.

I found the same company, and very soon heard the news that the widow was married to my friend the curate, two days before my return; and, as they had not got an house, my aunt had obliged him to be with her 'till one was put in order to receive them. I saluted, and very gravely wished her joy; and, as soon as I well could, took myself away to indulge my thoughts. I was shocked at her conduct —She appeared to me as an abandoned creature.

I was pleased to see Corinna come to me: *Pray, Madam,* I said, *was it too much trouble for you to have given me a line, that I might have been here time enough to have been at the wedding? Indeed,* she answered, *I knew nothing of it 'till it was over; they were married before any one in this family was made acquainted they intended it. Her fortune was at her own disposal, and her mother was a stranger to the courtship; and was not asked her consent 'till it was too late to refuse it, if it would have been regarded. I am satisfied,* I replied; *I see now how he came to take your denial so calmly—He had the widow in his eye. I wish he may be happy. So do I,* Corinna said; *but I greatly doubt it. I am afraid she is at heart a very bad woman. I fear she has too much exposed herself. But I can tell you, we have no room for you now—You are to lie at*

Farmer L—'s house. I am very glad of it, I answered; *but pray take care to send a bottle or two of something good there, that he and I may smoke a pipe together.*

Just then my friend came to us. He had been about some parish duty. I wished him joy, and he seemed fully satisfied both with his wife and her fortune. I begged of him, upon no account to tell his wife anything about Chloe and myself. He promised he would not, and was as good as his word.

In a short time their house was ready, and my friend took his wife and mother-in-law home, and I returned to my aunt's. I visited him constantly, and had every time more and more reason to think, with Corinna, *His wife was bad at heart.*

I was very uneasy I had no news from London. Indeed I concluded affairs were in the same posture I left them; but Chloe was continually in my mind, and the time approached when they generally came into the country. Mr. Trueman, I knew intended to carry Lucinda to his own seat; and, from what her father had said to him, I naturally enough imagined I should not be so welcome to Chloe's as before. I was not married, and he might reasonably wonder why I was not. I had not friendship to excuse my visits, because my friend would not be there. In short, to satisfy myself, I resolved to go to London for a few days.

CHAPTER XXVII

*The Author goes again to London.
Preparations making for Chloe's Wedding.
It is broke off. A Duel.*

This resolution was no sooner taken than executed, and I found my mind grow more easy, the nearer I approached to where Chloe resided. I went, according to his invitation and my promise, to Mr. Trueman, and found only Lucinda at home. She seemed very glad to see me, and said, *I have great news to tell you. Chloe is to be married within a few days. My papa says everything is agreed upon, and she seems perfectly easy—She looks like an angel—She went out just before you came.*

This a little staggered me. I could not doubt her, yet I could not reconcile her being at liberty, if she was to be compelled to the match. *You seem surprized,* she added: *but, I assure you, it is true.* I answered, *It was true her news greatly affected me—But may she be happy. I have no right to dispute her disposing of herself where she pleases.*

We were upon this subject, when we heard Mr. Trueman coming upstairs, and saying to somebody, *Indeed, Miss, you shall dine here. I will send word where you are*—When he entered with Chloe in his hand, and, seeing me, said, *So, Sir, are you here? I am glad to see you.* My thoughts were in a great deal of confusion; however I thanked him, and, making a low bow to Chloe, told her, I was very glad to see her look so well. She answered, with her usual sincerity, *I am very well; I am glad to see you so.*

My friend observing my uneasiness, and guessing the reason, took me to the window; and, speaking very low, told me not to give way to any suspicions, for I had no reason. This a little recovered my spirits. I waited impatiently for an opportunity to know the whole affair, and was not long without one; for Mr. Trueman, thinking we should want to be alone, found means to draw Lucinda out of the room.

Though we were alone, I was unable to speak to Chloe. My heart was too full, and we looked upon one another some time—When coming towards me, she said, *What ails you? what has Lucinda been saying to you!* I answered, taking her by both hands, *My dear angel, must I lose you? Is it come to that?* She replied, *No. What have I to do with the agreement among lawyers? I have given no consent. My mamma has ordered me to prepare for my wedding, and I am obeying her—Would you have had me to refuse? Assure yourself, if I find they are in earnest, the 'Squire will have his bride to seek.*

I begged her pardon, but told her I esteemed her too much to lose her without concern. *I believe you,* she said, *neither do I intend you shall. I am prepared for what may happen, and have sent a box agreeable to the direction you gave me. Your friend has engaged his honour to me that he would take care I should get safely away: That makes me so easy, and helps me to amuse them. My conduct pleases my mamma; and, I believe, she expects me to be a lady the day of my marriage. The 'Squire, I hear, is to be created a baronet. My father-in-law is against the match, and I cannot now fancy they are in earnest. He is very cunning; and, I imagine yet, all this is to sound my inclinations*—adding, *Are you easy now? What will make you easy?* I replied, embracing her, *Nothing but the possession of my charming Chloe.*

Mr. Trueman came into the room, and said, *I hope now all points are settled—The clouds I see are cleared up:* And turning to Chloe, *I have been talking with your father-in-law—He is gone home*

—Your match is over with the 'Squire. But I will not give you the pleasure now to tell you what has broke it off. Now for the Captain, Chloe—but Lucinda's coming in, prevented more. She too said the match was off—and wished Chloe joy, hinting, that though she had carried it so well between all parties, it never entered into her head that she intended to have him. *No, no, I cannot believe it,* she said—*this is the gentleman for you, I dare say, Chloe.* My friend prevented any explanations, and dinner coming up, we passed some hours very agreeably.

When Chloe went home, my friend said, *She will have it by and by; and I am sure, from what my father-in-law dropped, he does not intend she shall slip through his son's fingers—he will treat with no more squires..*

The next day, about two o'clock, I went to Chloe's. Her mother was more ceremonious than usual, and I could get no account how the match came to be broke off. I had only the satisfaction to have a hint from Chloe, that she would be in Hyde-Park next day at noon. I told Mr. Trueman, and he offered to go with me, saying, *I think it will be better for us to be together.* Accordingly we met her, and she informed us that when she left us and came home, she was told she must think no more of the 'Squire; he was a debauched creature, and he should not have her fortune to throw away upon his mistresses—My mama saying, *Chloe, when he visits you again; tell him I forbid him my house; and you from receiving his addresses. A filthy fellow! We have discovered his pranks now! My son-in-law has found him out.* I answered, *I would obey her; and accordingly, when he came yesterday, I delivered my commands with great punctuality. He absolutely denied what was charged upon him, but I told him my brother-in-law saw him. He was very short in taking his leave, only saying, Well, Miss, good-*

bye then.

I confess, I was greatly satisfied in her being thus rid of the man of fortune—His state made him formidable. Yet, I dare say, if Mr. Schemal had not had a son, his scandalous behaviour and bad company, would never have been an objection to his marriage; but something was to be caught at to break off with him decently, and make room for Lucinda's brother.

After we had walked about an hour, we left Chloe at her own door, and went home. Mr. Trueman told me, he made no doubt now but they would push the Captain's marriage as far as they could. *I am afraid,* he said, *they will not give her half the fair play they have done in this; but, if I can, I will be in their secrets. I think it would be proper for you to visit your retreat, and if anything material happens you shall know it. I will write to you to your aunt's; and, as it may be found necessary, our friend the curate will be ready either to come with you to town, or to the old officer's. I shall set out soon for my country-seat, and should be sorry to leave Chloe to herself. She will not know how to manage to get away.* I answered, I was greatly obliged to him, and would follow his advice.

The next day at dinner, we were greatly surprized with a noise from the mouths of a number of bawling wretches crying, "A full and true account of a duel fought this morning in Hyde-Park, between 'Squire Shallow and Captain Schemal." It had happened that my friend and I had ridden out early that morning, and had just returned. Lucinda, not expecting her husband, was at her father's. However, one of the servants informed us that there had been a duel; that the 'Squire was run through the body, and the Captain was gone off.

This was important news. A gentleman coming in, my friend said, I will step to Chloe's, and be back presently—Make free, call for everything you want. When he was gone, I inquired of the gentleman if he had heard anything of the affair, and could relate any particulars to be depended upon. He informed me that he had some knowledge of one of the 'Squire's friends, who had seen him since he was wounded; *For,* says he, *he is not dead—and he tells me that he passed the evening with him before the duel. That he seemed greatly vexed, and often damned Captain Schemal for a scrub, saying, He had hindered him from having the prettiest girl in the kingdom: That some of the company worked him up to write a challenge to meet in Hyde Park: That when they met, the 'Squire being but a very little acquainted with the sword, was run through a part of his body; and the Captain immediately mounted his horse, and rode off.*

In about an hour my friend returned, and, to the former account, added that the Captain had written a letter to his father, and had gone for Holland, 'til he received advice how the 'Squire did. I observed he was extremely vexed at something, for he could not any way disguise his passions.

The gentleman did not stay long after his return —When he began, *That silly girl, Lucinda, has ruined you. Her concern for her brother has occassioned her to tell almost all she knew—Chloe is crying—Lucinda is now heartily sorry for what she has done—But it is too late. I found my father-in-law and Chloe's mother in deep consultation; and, when I came away, was civilly desired not to bring you any more there—Chloe's mother saying, She would take care her daughter should not trouble my house. I could have been angry with Lucinda, but I considered her condition.*

I was shocked at this piece of unexpected news, but begged him not to take any notice to Lucinda of his displeasure. *She,* I said, *I have no doubt, is ignorant of the nature of duels, and concludes, if*

159

the 'Squire dies, her brother must be hanged. Well, he answered, *all may be well yet, if she has not discovered me to be the confidant. My father-in-law will not choose to break with me. Go out of town, and I will be punctual in giving you an account. I pity Lucinda's weakness, but it shall make me double diligent to serve you.*

I took my leave directly, fearing Lucinda's return, as I was not then so much in temper as to have treated her with that deference possibly I ought, and which the wife of my best friend demanded from me; only begging of Mr. Trueman to remember me to Chloe, if he was permitted to have an opportunity of seeing her. This he promised me to do.

I had enough now to employ my thoughts. When was I to see Chloe again? She now, to be sure, was almost a close prisoner; and upon the Captain's return, if the 'Squire did not die, she would be compelled to marry him. What Lucinda had told I was a stranger to; I only knew she had told enough to point me out to be the person, on whom Chloe's inclinations were fixed. I was marked out to be avoided by every servant, and might depend upon it all the care would be taken to prevent my communicating my thoughts to her. I saw her made a sacrifice of, without its being any way in my power to prevent it. How did I blame myself, for not having everything prepared in time? Had my retreat been ready, I might have had the charming creature with me, and bid defiance to their power—*My own negligence,* I cried, *has lost her! forever lost her! Fool that I am.*

Thus I tormented myself, 'till I reached the good old Colonel's, who seemed greatly affected at my relation. All my hopes rested only, upon Lucinda's not having mentioned her husband as privy to my love. My good friend thought my case desperate, saying, *I have experienced the power of a father—*

You will find a father-in-law's worse. He wants the affections, so natural to a parent. He will show Chloe no more regard, than in making her the instrument to bring an estate into his family. My dear girl's father only endeavoured to keep his daughter from me. Chloe's father-in-law will force her to another. His aim is not so much to prevent a match, as to make one. She is in his power—He is not afraid of you—He wants to make her his son's —he knows you cannot get at her.

Thus he fed a despair I was too fond of nourishing myself and had almost persuaded me into a firm belief of its being impossible for me ever to have her. I answered him, she was not yet married; and, 'till I was sure she was, I would not give her up: That I was sure Mr. Trueman would do all he could to prevent her being compelled: That my hopes would yet get the better of my despair, though I knew not upon what well to ground them: That my present visit to him, was to get him to go once more to the retreat with me, to see everything was ready, and to give my final directions: Adding, *If I must lose her, I will live there myself: The thought of its being intended for Chloe will be some satisfaction to me; her idea will be over with me, and we will be there at least in imagination—If they rob me of her, they cannot rob me of the remembrance of her. I cannot upbraid her; if she marries another, I am sure it will be by compulsion. Her bridal-bed will be a bed of tears; and, surely, if she weeps in the arms of an husband, I may well mourn the loss of such a wife.* Very pathetic, indeed! he replied: *Well, we will go tomorrow; but you are a cup too low now: Wine must help love, or you will be very indifferent company, I find—But we are all apt to be so at one time or another of our lives—I was once so myself, so I will excuse you.*

In the morning we walked over again to the Serjeant's, who told me, he had received two large

161

chests, and a handsome box and a parcel. I knew the chests were full of books, so let them alone. The parcel I opened, and found in it a key, and a letter from Chloe; in which she let me know she had taken care to send some things for herself, if she was to be compelled to marry the 'Squire, and assured me of her full resolution to come to me, rather than submit to be unhappy.

I said to the Sergeant, *This box I must entrust to the care of your wife; let her open it, and put the things in proper order: She knows better how to regulate them than I do.* He called her, and I was extremely pleased with her appearance. She seemed quite a good motherly woman, and carried the remains of features which might once have entitled her to the character of an handsome woman. Her discourse convinced me she had been well bred, and that added to my satisfaction. I signified to her the favour I had to ask of her, and she answered, *I will engage to do it in a proper manner.*

We left her to her employment, and took a walk in the garden, which we found in very good order, considering the Sergeant was the only person to do all the work in it. The Sergeant acquainted us that he was appointed gamekeeper to the gentleman, for whom things were so often left at his house. *I was very unwilling*, he said, *to accept the office; but he pressed me so much, that I could not refuse him. He has been greatly wronged by the former gamekeeper; indeed he kept poachers off very well, but it was only to have the more opportunity to poach himself. He was in contract with some of our higglers, and furnished them with so much game a week, according to the season. I have promised my master I will never sell his game, but fairly told him, I would not give myself the trouble to preserve it, unless I might have leave now and then to make a present of a brace of birds, or an hare, to a friend. This he agreed to, and I am now the second qualified person in this manor.*

When we had finished our business here, we went back to the Colonel's; and, about two days after, I set out for my aunt's, and had the pleasure, in a few days, to receive a letter from Mr. Trueman.

CHAPTER XXVIII

*A Letter from the Author's Friend.
Chloe's Confinement, etc.*

"*My dear Friend,*

I resolved with myself, upon what Chloe's mother said to me, to give them very little of my company. Just after you left, Lucinda came home very much dejected. However displeased I was with her, I assure you, I showed no resentment to her, nor asked her one question concerning what had passed. This conduct embarassed her more than a contrary one would have done. She expected I should have been angry; but, as I never had the least difference with her, I determined to keep my temper, and defer the first quarrel, if possible, to the last day of my life. I love her, and consider her as guilty only of an indiscretion which she was hurried into through her regard for her brother, and the imaginary danger he would be in if the 'Squire died.

"Finding I took no notice of her, she burst into tears, saying, *I have ruined Mr. A——. Where is he?* I answered, *Gone, I suppose, for good.* She went on, *What has my folly done! What has my folly done! Chloe, in regard for him, did all and said all she could to engage my affections to you. He never left you, when you were ill—He took all the care he could of you, to preserve your life for me—He will think me a monster of ingratitude—I have ruined him—My fear for my brother, and my hopes to see him in possession of Chloe's estate, have ruined Mr. A——. He now never can have Chloe —she is a close prisoner—The 'Squire is thought to be out of danger, and my papa is determined to marry Chloe to my brother as soon as he returns.*

You will hate me—I have ruined your friend, and deceived my own—I have blamed her—I have used her ill, for being faithful—Yet, I am sure, I could not have borne the loss of you—They are forever separated, and I am the unhappy creature who has occasioned their separation.

"You, my good friend, love—and will excuse me, if I could bear no more. I took her in my arms and kissed her, saying, *My dear Lucinda, be easy—The last words my friend said to me were to beg me to show no resentment to you—He imagined it was your love for your brother—You have done him no other injury, than, if he cannot have Chloe, he will have nobody. He is gone; but where, or how far his distraction may lead him, or into what extravagancies, I know not. I am forbidden to bring him with me to your father's—Chloe is not to come here—I do not forbid your going to your father, but I will not.* She replied, *I never mentioned you—They know nothing of your being acquainted with the love Mr. A— has for Chloe—But, if you will not go, I will not go—I will do no more mischief—I can never bear the sight of that generous girl—Chloe must despise me.*

"Thus we passed a week, she vexing, I soothing; and she expressed the utmost uneasiness, at finding no letter came from you—often saying, *No letter yet from Mr. A—! Who knows what his despair may have done?* At last my father-in-law called upon me, and expressed much wonder he had not seen me. I told him, I looked upon the forbidding Chloe my house, as forbidding me his. He replied, *Chloe's mother looks upon you as an immediate party in Mr. A—'s interest, and imagines you knew of the love between them; and, as she is resolved not to give her daughter to him, she only endeavoured to prevent their having any meetings.* I am greatly obliged to her, I answered; and, that she may be under no uneasiness upon my account,

165

or under any fear of either myself or Lucinda's carrying on any correspondence between them, we have resolved to stay away. My friend is gone—We are going soon into the country—and you may be very easy. We shall rejoice at my brother's happiness. However, as he did not choose to break with me, he insisted upon our coming to dine there the next day.

"In hopes of seeing Chloe I went. Lucinda told me that she would make it up with her, and do all she could to serve you. When we came, I saw Chloe indeed; but she threw such a look of disdain at Lucinda, as pleased me. I admired her spirit—She seemed to assume courage, as if she had taken some desperate resolution. I was fearful she would do herself some injury, and just found time to tell her to trust Lucinda. She looked at me very earnestly, but took my advice.

"After dinner the women withdrew, and my father-in-law began about the obstinacy of his daughter-in-law, and how wrong it was to love without parents' consent. I answered, I knew no more of the matter, than that you were acquainted with her before I ever saw you: That it was owing to that acquaintance I had his daughter: That, in regard to you, I thought you fully deserved her, if merit could: That I never observed any more than the greatest respect from you to her; and, as you were gone, and where you might be I knew not, as I had not heard from you, I thought it seemed a very extraordinary step to keep an heiress a close prisoner, on purpose to force her to a marriage against her inclinations: That I was sure you would not want friends nor money, and there was a power would give her leave to choose another guardian; for, in point of fortune, the difference is not sufficient between my brother-in-law and my friend to determine an equitable judge in favour of either —*And you are sensible,* I said to him, *if it comes to that, they will not consent to any marriage 'till she is of age, unless to a man of equivalent fortune.* This a little startled him, and he answered, *She is only prevented from running away, but I will persuade her mother to give up her trust.* I confess, I did not believe him, but replied, I thought it would be right.

"When we returned home, I found Lucinda and she had partly made it up. As I am suspected and Lucinda is not, and assures me she will let me into all their schemes, I hope yet to see you together. Chloe has more liberty. Escuse this long epistle—I thought it proper to let you know all, and am

Yours sincerely,

John Trueman."

This was cordial news. Lucinda, I was sure, could do much, and my friend, and that was sufficient for me, had assured me she would. I now had an additional reason for my hopes. I had some grounds to bid despair be gone. I endeavoured to persuade myself all would yet be right. I knew my own income would keep us well, at my little hovel.—*I have never yet*, I said to myself, *valued or considered her fortune. We shall have enough for decency, and love must supply the place of grandeur. We shall neither hear scandal, nor give occasion for it. We shall have no promises to break, nor interests to pursue. We shall have nothing to be proud of but our love, and, consequently, can treat no inferior with insolence. My horses will splash no man of honour, nor will the sauciness of her chairmen turn one woman of merit into the dirt.*

I reflected, in that retirement, if I could do no good, I was absolutely prevented from doing harm, and contented myself with musing on real happiness. Corinna and the curate were now my confidants. They were valuable friends, and sincere in their professions—They meant what they said. My aunt declined apace; and at her death, I might have everything in my power to make my retirement agreeable to Chloe.

I kept nothing secret from these friends but my little house. I could not bring myself to trust that spot to the knowledge of too many—My treasure was to be there, and I was a real miser.

I was in this temper when a letter came to my aunt. She kept the contents, contrary to her custom, very secret. She seemed displeased at something, and took a great deal of consideration to regulate her proceedings. Corinna and I observed it; but, with all our penetration, we could not discover the old gentlewoman's drift: However, at last it came out. My aunt sent for me, and began thus—*I cannot expect to live long, and you are not insensible that I have long designed to see you married to my god-daughter. She is a good girl— You are my nephew—My fortune is left between you. As I decline apace, I will be at the wedding, and expect your compliance one day within this fortnight. I will speak to Corinna—See you both obey me.*

I bowed and retired. This was a home-stroke— No art could divert this—No equivocation would serve now. I knew her temper—She had given us time enough to court, and had reason to expect our compliance. I said to Corinna, *My dear Corinna, let the storm fall upon me. I must deny—You may show a ready obedience. I cannot make you happy —You know my situation.*

Accordingly, when she was spoken to, she answered that she was all obedience. But why unnecessary preparations, for what I never intended to perform? I even resolved at once to tell the truth. My aunt had once loved, and who could tell? She might pity me; but, instead of pity, I raised a storm. *So then,* she said, *it is true. I have been made a property of! My house was convenient to visit an heiress from; and, under a pretended courtship to my god-daughter, you carry on intrigues elsewhere. Be gone! Quit my house—You shall know how much I resent it—But poor Corinna, she loves you—I am sure she does—Well, my favours shall make her amends for the slight you put upon her love.*

Excuses were all in vain, and I kindly took leave of Corinna, desiring her to send my things to such an inn in town; and, having received a promise from my friend the curate that he would come anywhere to me at a minute's warning, I set out once again for London—having first had the pleasure of reading the contents of the letter, which maliciously enough was intended to do, and did all the mischief. It was from Chloe's mother, and set forth the great regard children ought to have to their parents and relations; and, out of that principle, she had taken the liberty to acquaint her that she had reason to imagine I was deceiving her; and that I, in reality, courted her daughter, while I amused her with pretending courtship to Corinna—That the only way to be satisfied was to press my marriage; and my denial or compliance would evince the truth—That she had taken such measures that I might be assured I never should have Chloe.

Very well, I thought, that mine is sprung, and I may have a chance to know more soon. I resolved I would not go to my friend's, nor to my usual inn, but send a porter with a note to him, acquainting him where I was. This I immediately did upon my quitting my horse, and the man was so lucky as to meet him coming out of his own house. He read it, and said, *I will be there presently;* and came in a few minutes after the porter.

I informed him how I had been treated at my aunt's, from the letter Chloe's mother wrote. *Oh,* he said, *that is my wife's father-in-law's doing. They want to see you married, for at present they are at a loss how to proceed with Chloe—She is indeed pretty much watched. Lucinda says her brother is every day expected in town again; that some scheme is a-foot which I shall know, if they let her into the secret. In the meantime, I think it will be right for you to keep close—I will call upon you, and you must regulate your measures by theirs.* I answered him, that I would do so; but, as I did not think I should have any farther occasion for my horse, desired he would take him again. *No, no,* he replied, *that will never do, let him be sold: If I have him, they will naturally conclude I know something of you—I will let you know how things go.*

Accordingly, some days after, I sent my horse to Smithfield, directing the man to say he had bought it at Oxford. In a few hours he returned, and told me he had sold him to an officer for twenty-five guineas. When my friend came to me, I acquainted him with it: *I knew it,* he answered, *Lucinda's brother bought him; and it is a matter of triumph among them, that you are obliged to sell your horse. There has been a quarrel about you—Your aunt has returned an answer to the letter, wherein she tells them that, to show her resentment for your double proceeding upon your refusal to marry Corinna, she has ordered you out of her house, and intended to put you out of her will: Adding, "He is gone to the University, and there let him stay; for, unless he consents to marry Corinna, he shall never come here again." This gave them great satisfaction, and Chloe was called to read the letter. "Well, daughter," her mother said, "will you marry a beggar?" Chloe replied, She might, she imagined, thank them for it, if you were one—That she would not be behind you in constancy, saying, "If he can refuse beauty and fortune for me, I can easily refuse a Captain for him." This has nettled them, and, Lucinda tells me, they are preparing to go into the country, having resolved to compel Chloe to marry her brother. I have told her you are in town, and expect her to call upon me.*

In a little time Lucinda came in a hackney chair. She behaved extremely open, telling me she should never forgive herself if I lost Chloe—That she only was to blame, but she would make me all the amends in her power. I replied, *Then, Madam, as you are admitted to the sight of the fair prisoner, you will oblige me greatly in conveying a billet to her. With all my heart,* she said, *and will engage also to bring you back an answer.* Upon this assurance, I wrote the following note to Chloe.

"*My dear Chloe,*

I am happy in having intelligence how you are used, and how you are designed to be used—I will use the utmost means to prevent their schemes. I would advise you to give way to them a little, for fear they should hasten your marriage. I can better free you in the country than here. I keep quite private, and no one but my friend, and the bearer of this, knows I am in town. Be careful of your health.

My Life! My Soul!

Adieu."

I gave this to Lucinda, and about two days after had the pleasure of seeing her again. She delivered me a note, saying, *I have faithfully executed my commission, and bring you this from Chloe.*

"SIR,

Lucinda greatly surprized me by bringing me your note. We are perfectly reconciled—I am very well—You may depend upon my keeping my resolution—I depend upon your assistance.

Yours,

Chloe."

Lucinda, after I had read the note, told me, she could hardly persuade Chloe to trust her with an answer—*Not but she had reasons for suspecting me,* she said, *and very good ones—But we are now friends. In about a week they go into the country, and my papa has taken out a licence. He says, "Her crying and pouting shall avail her little." The cousin is to marry them.*

So, thought I, the scheme is deeply laid, and her refusal will be of little consequence. If they marry her immediately upon their getting into the country, my assistance will signify nothing—*Poor Chloe, you must be sacrificed! It is out of my power to help you!* Lucinda saw my concern, and said, *I am the occasion of all this.*

When she was gone, I resolved to go to the Colonel's again, and keep quite close, 'till I had some account how affairs stood; and, had not Mr. Trueman called upon me, I had abruptly done so, without ever thinking of getting the curate to me. He told me they set out such a day, and advised me to be there before them, and have our friend ready, saying, *If I can find the least opportunity to get Chloe out, I will bring her to you.*

I immediately wrote to the curate a circumstantial account, and desired him to come, with all the privacy he could, to the Colonel's to me—which he did the day before they came into the country. I was very uneasy to hear something from the family, but we dared not stir out. The third day Mr. Trueman came, and informed us the Captain had broken his arm: It was a little uncharitable, but I could not help wishing he had broken his neck. *Your horse, says he, flung him. He rode him with a bit and furniture; and the creature, not being used to such a manner, threw him about five miles off. He got him so far, though he was in danger of being off several times. This defers Chloe's execution a little; but as I am certain she cannot escape him, unless she consents to run away as soon as she can, I will get her out and see her married, and then you must manage as you can.*

The Colonel said, *Sir, you are a worthy gentleman, and I believe think as I do; it is pity to part them. He deserves her, if anybody deserves her. He is a gentleman without an estate; she is a young lady who, if she lives, will have a good one: And, I think, the difference of five hundred pounds a year between the Captain and him ought not to be considered so far as to force her inclinations.* Mr. Trueman answered, *Sir, though he is my brother-in-law, I will not sacrifice my friend to a family interest—There are young ladies enough fond of a red coat—But, as Chloe was pre-engaged, I will give her my assistance to bring her to the man she loves. They imagine my friend here to be at Oxford, and his affairs too desperate, by the loss of his aunt's favour, to attempt anything to disturb them. They know he cannot come to the house, and they take all the care they can—that Chloe shall receive no letters.*

When he was gone, I was upon the rack—fearful one moment, full of hope the other. I was sure, if I had her not now, I never could have her. Thus I passed my time in agonizing uneasiness—When the second morning after my friend had been here, he entered—and with him Chloe.

I ran to her, saying, *My dear Chloe! We will part no more! Indeed but you will*, he answered. *I have brought her out, and I will see her home. I must return to London this afternoon—You know Lucinda's condition. I will give Chloe away, according to my promise, and leave the rest to her management. I will be no farther in the secret.*

The curate was there, and the ceremony soon over. *You are now mine!* I said: *My dear angel! When am I to expect you?* She softly answered, *Be ready to receive me, I will take the first opportunity.*

My good friend the Colonel came gaily to her, saying, *Madam, I kissed you when you was Miss Worthy, give me leave now to kiss Mrs. A—. I wish you joy from my heart. I am sure my friend will use you according to your merit.* She behaved with great resolution, only saying, *If I am guilty of disobedience, impute it to my love.* Mr. Trueman hurried her away, and left me bewildered in my thoughts. It seemed another dream—another pleasing, gay illusion.

The Colonel, seeing I was quite absent, hit me a slap on the shoulder, saying, *What, are you sorry you are married? Come, raise your spirits; take off a bumper of old hock to her health. I will have no port today. I will examine my cellar, and make libations of the best to love and marriage.*

In the afternoon the curate departed, Mr. Trueman having, in the morning, given him fresh assurances of serving him, as soon as he could. I had told him, he might trust Corinna with my marriage; and, if anything material should happen, to send me a line, under cover, to my good friend. He was scarce gone when the Serjeant entered. *I am glad to see you*, I said; *you are the very man I wanted. The business is done, but I cannot tell to an hour or a day, when we shall be with you.* He answered, *All shall be ready; come when you will, you shall not wait a minute at the door.* I thanked him, and my old friend said, *I will warrant for him—He has been used to be awake—But she will scarce come this afternoon: Push about the flask—the claret is good. Come, Serjeant, drink to the happy couple, and fill your pipe. You will like your guests—I never saw a young lady behave with more spirit in my life—I hate your affected ones—She seemed pleased to give a proof of her love.*

We were thus dedicating the evening to joy—when I started up—*By G—, there she goes! Home! Home, Serjeant, as fast as you can! Where! Where!* says the Colonel. *Yonder! I am sure it is she!* I answered—*She steers for the Serjeant's—I will run and meet her—She is right not to come here.*

Away I flew—Cupid lent me his wings—and, in a little time, I met her in some closes she was obliged to go through. *My dear Chloe!* I cried. She replied, *This is no time for compliments!—Away!*

I conducted her safe to her retreat, without meeting or seeing one person. She was no sooner set down in her parlour, than she burst into a violent fit of crying—saying, every now and then, *What have I done! What have I done!* I thought it would be best to let this sudden gust of passion have way a little, only now and then saying, *My dear, compose yourself—Compose yourself, my dear Chloe.*

In a little time it was over, and she entirely came to herself. *My joy overpowered me,* she said—*I could scarce believe I was got here.* I inquired of her, how she got away so soon? She replied, *When your friend was gone, my good cousin and my mamma set down to backgammon, and my father-in-law was to take up the conqueror. I went into the garden, and walked up and down in sight for an hour or more, to amuse them, if they should have any suspicion of me; but, I believe, they had none. I observed the garden-door next the fields was open, the gardener being busy in wheeling out some stuff he had been clearing away. At last, observing him to go into the house, it came into my head now was my time; and, without any hesitation, I made the best of my way across the great field, into the closes. I had some notion where the haunted house was; but I owe more to good luck, and your meeting me, than to any certainty I was in to find it.*

I told her that as my mind was full of her, I often threw my eyes towards their house, though I had no expectations of her coming so soon—That I saw her fly along, and ran down the lane to meet her, concluding she had found means to give them the slip. She answered, looking tenderly at me, *All this I have done for you. But my poor mamma—I pity my poor mamma—Her heart will relent when she finds I am gone.*

The Serjeant came in, and hindered her saying more. *You are just in time, Madam,* he said; *for you was soon missed. I saw the gardener—He was sent one way after you—They are all out upon the search for you. He asked me if I had seen a young lady go by me any where within this hour in my walk? I replied, No, none had been near me; but, when I was upon the hill, I saw two people at a distance, seemingly in great haste, going towards E——; but I was not near enough to distinguish who they were. They are them, to be sure, he cried; and made the utmost expedition after them. If I had not put him upon a wrong scent, he must have got sight of you upon the common; but now, I am sure, you are safe.*

We assured him we were greatly obliged to him, and we would make him sensible of it, desiring him to get us some supper, and we should expect him and his wife to bear us company.

It seemed to me to be very lucky for us that this man had been made a game-keeper, as he would have opportunities to hear what the report of the country was concerning us, while he only appeared to be about his business. My dear Chloe and I were now again alone—She was now my wife, and permitted me, without relectance, to press numberless kisses on her roseate lips. My love had been starved; and the delicacy, so commendable in Miss Worthy, would have been troublesome in Mrs. A—. This pressing courtship warmed her, and I saw love glowing on her cheeks, and desire kindling in her eyes, when my good landlady entered with a couple of fine fowls boiled.

We could scarce prevail on her and her husband to bear us company; but, however, we supped together, and everything was as neat as we could wish. I inquired of my landlord what company he had came to him? And desired him to direct us how to regulate our conduct that we might avoid being seen. He told us, it was but seldom anybody called, but we might easily be apprized when they did: That his outer door was generally locked, and he would take care to give us time to retire before he opened it to anyone: That no one came after dark —*Well then*, says I, *we must make supper our best meal, for it will not be proper to have any extraordinary cooking about. Go on your old way and we will take a bit of anything and a glass of wine at noon, and have something dressed at night.*

Thus we chatted away time, 'till I observed to Chloe it grew near one. I had taken notice that she often cast her eye upon her watch; and, I sincerely believe, was sorry to see time move so fast. I saw her timidity, and, taking her by the hand said, *My dear Chloe, will you retire?*

With what transports of delectable expectation did I open the door to the chamber that, tonight, my Chloe and I would share as husband and wife! The dear girl's nervousness was entirely visible in the manner her hand shook as she reached out to accept the glass of wine I proffered. We sipped two glasses of it apiece and nibbled some sugared Italian biscuits, thus postponing the sweet moment when Chloe and I would at last be one.

The spirits seemed to soothe the tremours in my Chloe's soul and when I, putting down my glass for the last time, stepped to her and embraced her closely to my bosom, she fitted her body to mine with such sweet tranquility that I fairly swooned.

Kissing her gently parted lips, I felt with my hand the softness of her cheek, now aglow with a bewitching blush. I followed with my fingers the delicate curve of her forehead to her hair, which I set free from its imprisoning ribbon, letting the soft burnished curls tumble in careless cascade to her shoulders. I buried my face in those delightful locks, wishing to feel with more exactitude their warmth and to inhale the sweet scent of my Chloe's own perfumes.

Still sensing a shyness in my fair bride, I did not fail to make the most soothing expressions of endearment, the most sincere assurances of the depth of my love to allay the maiden's fears.

Never repent, my darling Chloe, the boldness of the decision you have taken, I whispered. She assured me of the fidelity of her passions and the truth of her own very deepest love for me. No husband could have wished more. She was the object of my fiercest wishes, my most extravagant passions. My pulses raced with longing, flurrying amidst a flush of the now surfacing desires I had so long put from my mind. I struggled between my feelings of the utmost tenderness and my sensations of the most demanding and violent sensuality. I held my Chloe so fast to my breast that she gasped.

I released her, kissing her again, allowing my hungry lips to travel down to the warm spot in her throat where the twin pulses raced in uneven tempo.

My impatience to possess the one who had occupied my dreams impelled me to lift the dear one, my lips still pressed upon hers, to the waiting bed. Gently, so as not to distress the tender sentiments I saw reflected in her eyes, I unloosed my Chloe's gown and, her passions keeping pace with my own, she unfastened the stays and lay back, her lovely body but barely concealed by the near transparent shift. I made haste to remove my own shirt and breeches, and seeing Chloe's hand move toward the fastenings at the bodice of her shift, I helped her to undo them—and to remove the last hindrance to my first sight of that body for which I had so long suffered in denial.

Oh! What wondrous beauty! What rapturous divinity!

Her bosom, now bare, was rising in the warmest throbs and presented to my eyes the firm swell of young breasts, such as must be imagined on the most beautiful of goddesses. Their whiteness, their delicate fashioning, were all that man had ever dreamed of in his most fantastical imaginings. Their rosy nipples, surmounting the pale mounds of taut flesh, added the final ravishment to my eye and the most exquisite of pleasures to my roaming hands. She lay there silent, unresisting of the examination of her body by my love-filled eyes and my pleasure-ravished hands. Her tender acquiescence to my probings encouraged me to pursue to completion my long-held goal.

Taking her small hand in mine, I guided it down to my rod which had by now stretched himself to a fair tallness. The head was extended and blushed a fiery crimson showing the rush of hot blood to its tip. Chloe gasped, pulled away for an instant, then sighed as I placed her sweet hand firmly around the erect shaft, by now springing up straight from the wreath of curls that lay at its base. She held her hand still, then by my tender encouragement began to stroke the member softly. Anon, with great fearfulness, she reached her hand down to its base, lingered there in the curly thicket and thence strayed down to the spherical treasure-bed that Nature suspended between my thighs. I knew the softness of her fingers as she felt with wonder that globe of wrinkled flesh that held the honey of passion's flowering. Her hand clung to the root of my first instrument, that part in which Nature contained the stores of pleasure and I made her feel distinctly, through the soft outer cover, the pair of round balls that seemed to float within.

The visit of her warm hands to those impassionable parts had raised my desires to a boiling heat and I, near to overflowing with ungovernable passions, set upon the attainment of my goal.

Her thighs were already open to my love assaults in obedience to the irreversible laws of Nature. I lowered myself between them, and for the first time did the hard bone of my instrument feel the wiry curls that hid Chloe's full-pouted lips. Pressing on, that instrument drove at her breech, conformed to the dictates of Nature, yet shielded over with Nature's own device. I pushed vigorously, yet came against a wall which would not open to admit me.

With a soft moan, my Chloe complained.

She could not bear it.... *You hurt me, husband,* she murmured in pain.

Ah! conflict of my feelings!

Once more I essayed entry, gently, tenderly. Yet it did not avail me. The scimitar of flesh forbade me penetration. These fruitless attempts yielded nought but cries of anguish from my beloved Chloe. But she did not complain; she did not rail against the husband who was the first man ever to press to serve her so.

I begged my Chloe, my wife, to bear with patience. I reached a pillow beneath her buttocks, thus to make a point-blank aim at the most favourable elevation. Again I lowered myself between

Chloe's spread thighs, and rested the tip of my machine against that tiny cleft. So small was the slit that I could scarce count upon the accuracy of my aim. But assuring myself, I stroked forward with violent energy. My rod's immense stiffness surged forth with implacable fury, wedged against, then rent, the seal that had denied me access. This furious stroke gained me entrance to the tip alone; but following well the initial insertion, I once stroked again vigorously and aggressively, increasing the advantage just gained. Inch by inch, achieved with violent thrusts, I was at last in possession of that treasured prize.

At long last freed from the demands of my own throbbing loins, I looked into my Chloe's face and saw that she had pushed the sheet into her mouth to prevent her disturbing the house with her cries of pain. I gently removed the cloth and kissed her lips.

Now deep inside her, the fury of my passion drove me to complete the journey on which I had started forth with such difficulty. I thrust and stroked, heedless of the pain it caused the darling virgin. With an immense shudder, my liquids burst forth from me. As I withdrew my slackening member, I saw that the love-froth was tinged with blood and that Chloe had fainted with the anguish of the tremendous onslaught.

Carefully and gently I used the sheet to mop the stream of blood that flowed from her pleasure-wounded channel.

When she returned to her senses, she caressed and kissed me tenderly, explaining that I need not regret the pain that I had caused her. It was, she told me, the obligation of love; and its experience, proof of our love.

Sweat-drenched and fatigued, we fell into a gentle sleep, our arms wrapped close around one other.

I who had murdered her virginity slept deep and

dreamless and she, the victim of my passion, whimpered tenderly in her dreams.

I awoke later in the night and once more desired entrance. But I knew that that part of her must be so inflamed that I resisted and we slept on through the night.

In the morning, our landlady came to know our pleasure about our breakfast. I let her in, and went down into the garden to her husband. When I saw all things were ready, I went to fetch Chloe down.

At my entrance into our chamber, she met me with great tenderness in her looks, and said, *Can you contentedly dwell here with me?—The prisoners of love. Assure yourself I can—My thoughts rove not beyond this sweet retreat*, I answered. *My dear Chloe never suspected me before marriage; and, she may assure herself, I will give her reason after—I can live here, with you, in content for ages —Happy in you, I have no wish, nor give one thought beyond these walls.*

After breakfast she had employment enough to look over her drawers, that she might know where to find everything she might want. My good landlady, according to a laudable custom in the country, had scented all the linen with dried roses and lavender. We then opened the chests, and Chloe was pleased to be in possession of such a collection of books, saying, *Would any person who saw the outward appearance of this place imagine it to be so elegantly furnished within?—You have been too expensive.*

These matters being all regulated, I was more happy than thousands. I was master of a well-ordered family—My landlord acted as my butler, his wife as my cook; and, when supper was served up, were my companions. I had no *valet de chambre* indeed to pry into my secrets, and betray them— No luxury to encourage—Hot everyday was all that was required. His yard afforded fowls; his gun, game—In love only extravagant.

We spent the afternoons at our ease in our chamber, Chloe resting; I diligently applying myself to my books.

One afternoon, whilst contentedly passing the time thus, I chanced to look up from my studies and saw Chloe, reclining in bed, all naked, her body glowing with the dew of youth. I passed over to her and, kissing her shoulder, murmured words of love.

Immediately my member, responding to impulses deep within me, begins to transform himself into the stiff gristle of *amour*. I kiss Chloe again, she responding the more ardently. She wraps her arms around my neck, thus allowing me the freedom to undo the laces that close my shirt and, at length, to remove my breeches.

I slip into the bed, already warmed by her pulsing body. Slowly I begin to make advances toward my adored wife, when she takes me by surprize— moving abruptly and lowering herself upon my member, by now extended to his fullest proportion. Following her impulse, she runs the slit of her Venus-mound directly upon the flaming point of my sword, thus piercing herself through the center and infixing herself upon it to the extremest degree. Thus she sets upon me, straddling me with her open thighs.

I, in delight, pulled her down to receive the token of my kisses, at the same time increasing the rising sting of pleasure. I toyed with her pert breasts thus arousing her to a sweet storm of wriggles which apace aroused my own sensations.

Up and down she moved, in the inverted position of mortar and pestle. And she then swayed herself from side to side thus extending even further the arena of our mutual enjoyments. The volleys of heaves and counter-thrusts increased to a violent rhythm over which neither of us had any more control. In anticipation of the ultimate moment, I pulled my Chloe down over me with a fevered emotion and, in an instant, we both discharged, flowing mightily from within, the one on the other.

I lay back, so overcome was I with the ecstasy of the moment; and Chloe, inflamed to an intolerable point, lifted herself off my still-erect weapon and sank down on to the bed, stretching her love-moist body against my own, also wet with the exudations of passion.

We remained thus, silent, for some time.

When, presently, my Chloe sighed, I shut her complaining lips gently with a humid kiss. I had thought myself exhausted from the previous exertions and was extravagantly surprized to feel with those light kisses the stirring in my organ of bliss. And Chloe, too, responded, her thighs shifting restlessly. I made free with my hand, partaking with leisure of the joys of her firm body. They roved unchecked by any demur on her part and, by such manipulations were we both soon again at a high point of mutual fever.

Chloe's thighs, by now obedient to the inclinations of both Nature and passion, happily opened, and with a glad submission, offered up that tender, ruby gateway to the portal of pleasure. The velvet tip of my aroused organ met the deliciousness of her secret haven. I entered her, inch by inch, to the utmost of my length and, for some sweet moments, remained there, my sword impaling her.

She embraced love's arrow in eager, dear suction round it, compressing it inwardly. Every fibre of her love bowl strained to to be conjoined with my weapon of love. We gave pause, the better to delight in the sweetness afforded in that most intimate point of union. But the impatience inevitable to such a position soon made itself felt—and drove us to the mightiest action.

I drove into her with a fierce tumult and she

responded with the most violent rejoinders. The more insistent, the more furious became my action, the more heartfelt and frenzied her re-actions.

Oh happiest of all mortals! We were joined in that most *intime* of all positions. The rhythm increased to a superhuman intensity: and my body, suffused with the boiling blood of passion, convulsed itself with the agitation of my ultimate rapture. My discharge, which I had thought would be diminished by the previous exertions seemed only to be redoubled. And, Chloe's discharge similarly seemed to be amplified by such previous encounter and we were near drowned in the waves of liquid sweets which emanated with the immensest force from our bliss-parts.

We lay back, she in a pallour of faint and I, almost beyond the reaches of my mind in delight. Thus satisfied beyond the capacities of our most extravagant dreams, we slept, our arms entwined, our thighs wrapped around each other so that our intimate parts were in conjunction.

We had been here about ten days when the Colonel called in upon us. The pleasure of seeing each other was sincere. He informed us that the pursuit had been very hot; *But you know*, he said, *to no purpose. It is imagined you are concealed in London, but how you got there puzzles them. Every inn, every public house in this part were examined; but no one had been at any of them, answering the description given of you. In particular, Madam, I have this to say to you,* addressing himself to Chloe: *Your father-in-law called upon me, and inquired, as he said he was informed I was acquainted with your husband, if I had lately seen him. I answered he was at my house such a day, but left me very hastily at the close of the evening.*

"The scheme was settled then long before," he replied; "and she is certainly gone with that beggar: *Though, had it not been for the accident of my*

son's breaking his arm, I had disappointed them—
She might have eloped, if she would, after she had
been married. I wish though I could catch him; he
should lie in jail 'till his wife was of age."

Chloe reddened, and said, *I am greatly obliged to
him for his good opinion of me—Elope!—I should
never have thought of that. Had I been forced to
marry his son, I could have wept my misfortune, but
still should have thought it my duty to have continued a faithful wife. They convince me it was not
me, but my fortune that the father and son both
aimed at. I am pleased I had the resolution to
choose the alternative of making myself happy,
instead of giving them the power to make me miserable.*

Madam, replied my friend, *hear me out. I let him
know a little of my mind; fairly telling him I had a
great opinion of this gentleman's merit—That I
knew there was a mutual liking between you to
each other—That without derogating from his
son's merit, as fortune was out of the question on
either side, your inclinations ought to have been
considered; Adding, "You, Sir, broke off a match
between a man of fortune and your daughter-in-
law, giving for reason a piece of folly he had been
guilty of in London, when you know he had long
before been guilty of the same in the country, at
the beginning of his addresses to Miss Worthy." He
began to grow warm, and I as warm; when he left
me, with saying, "I find there is a confederacy
against me, but I will be as cunning as any of you."
I since learn, Madam, the father-in-law's resentment prevails over the mother's tenderness. She
would have been glad to have seen you, and to have
been reconciled to you; often saying, "I occasioned
everything to make him agreeable—I should have
thought the girl was not insensible—I miss my
Chloe." But those emotions are over; and, you may
assure yourself, if her husband can preserve the*

ascendancy he now has, you will neither one or other have any favour at their hands, farther than they can help.

Chloe answered directly, *I love my mamma—I would crawl upon my knees to receive her blessing—But, if anger has driven away tenderness; if a bad passion is substituted in the room of a good one, here I transfer every affection, and will double my love, to make confinement sit easy upon the man I chose.* This received a tender answer from me, expressed really from my heart.

Time passed agreeably, and we had often the pleasure of my good friend's company. Chloe and I passed our hours more happy than imagination could well suggest. I found in that dear girl an inclination to books, and a surprizing judgment in what she read—She was an inexhaustible fund of knowledge—Her observations were just—We had no care upon us—Five or six months rolled away, as so many weeks, for the hours of love fly swift—When, to my great satisfaction, I found she was breeding—And, about this time, my landlord brought me a letter from Corinna.

"SIR,

By the inquiry made after you, I was almost sure of your being in possession of your Chloe. My aunt has died exasperated against you. I am her heir, she having left everything, except five hundred pounds to you, to me.—She was pleased to say you should not starve. Your friend the curate has left the country, being presented to a good living by the gentleman who was once here with you. As I must be unhappy, for the real loss of you is insupportable, I shall soon quit the scene of my guilty correspondence with you.

"The person who manages my affairs will pay the money to your order. I have desired him to answer your draught at once as I imagine you do not at present choose to be seen—Wherever I am you will be in my thoughts, and if you should ever want my assistance I feel I have too much tenderness for you to deny it. I knew not of your marriage 'till your friend left the country about four days ago—He made an apology for keeping it a secret from me confessing he had your liberty to disclose it to me sooner. He said he had obliged his friends in doing what they asked of him; but he could not consent to tell anyone he married you for fear of the resentment of Chloe's family—It was a secret of consequence. I wish you joy and wish you happy. I shall take as much care to conceal myself as you have done—Make your draught upon Mr. D—, in R—, and he will answer it.

*I am yours,
The unhappy
Corinna.*"

I acquainted Chloe with no more of the contents of this letter than what related to the death of my aunt and my legacy observing an inviolable secrecy in regard to what had passed between Corinna and myself. I had before received the pleasure to hear Lucinda had brought my friend a son—That all were well; but that, upon a notion of his being privy to my match with Chloe, all correspondence was at an end between the two families—My friend concluding, with saying, *They write not now to me nor I to them. The loss of Chloe's fortune mortified my father-in-law too much, that, imagining, I was accessory to her marriage with you, he forgets to treat his daughter with common civility; and I hear, from other hands, that his resentment is so great against you for frustrating his golden schemes, that he will never permit a reconciliation to be made between Chloe and her mother. I know his temper so well that Chloe must not flatter herself with the hopes of one farthing more than they can help.*

This news was not at all disagreeable to me. I had enough—I had no expenses abroad, nor company at home to devour my income—My desires centered only in Chloe; and Chloe was with me—busy in preparing everything against the good time. I attended her with a fond and constant assiduity. I said everything I could to convince her how dear she was to me, and to make her burden as light as possible. The violence of passion settled into a perfect and mutual esteem for each other.

But this happy tranquillity was soon to be disturbed—A fever seized the charming girl and a thousand fears me. I sent for our good friend the Colonel, acquainting him with her illness. He made haste to me, bringing with him his apothecary. I soon saw he apprehended her distemper would be fatal. My condition is more easily to be judged than expressed. I kissed her parched lips, in hopes of communicating her illness to myself. I had no wish beyond her recovery, but that of dying with her—However, I was not so lost to thought as to neglect sending for every assistance.

I sent for her cousin. He was greatly surprized at seeing her so ill, and at finding how safely we had secured ourselves to elude inquiry. He seemed touched with my grief, and said he would endeavour to bring her mother to her. Chloe said, *Dear Sir, do—I long to see my mamma.*

The next day he came again, and said to Chloe, *Madam, your mother has empowered me to give you her blessing and her forgiveness, but I cannot prevail upon her to see you.* She answered, *I am obliged to her—I was prepared for the worst that might happen there—But here I am unprepared—* And, taking me by the hand, with the utmost tenderness, said, *How can I think of parting with you? Oh! that we could die together!*—And, drawing me close to her, expired.

Thus died Chloe—the lovely, the amiable Chloe—In the pride of youth, and the full bloom of beauty. In her personal accomplishments, equalled by few; in the sincerity of her love, excelled by none.

My good old friend and her cousin forced me out of the room, and kindly used every argument to compose me—They knew my loss was great—But no arguments could prevail upon me to quit my retreat. I kept there for years, visiting only my friend the Colonel, 'till he also resigned his breath, leaving me in his will particular, and very singular proofs of the truth of that friendship he had so long professed for me.

Indeed, I had a secret pleasure in my retirement—Chloe was ever in my thoughts—She lived in my memory—I encouraged no other ideas, but such as were fraught with the beauty, the truth, and the tenderness of Chloe.

I spent many watchful nights, in vain hopes of having the dear angel's company, 'till the warning cock had summoned her from me. Life would, even now, be insupportable, were it not from a full assurance of once more meeting with, and never more being separated from, ALL I EVER LOVED, OR EVER SHALL, CHLOE.

Let our melancholy story admonish parents from FORCING THE INCLINATIONS OF THEIR CHILDREN; and teach youth THAT OBEDIENCE TO THEIR PARENTS LAYS THE FOUNDATION FOR CERTAIN HAPPINESS:

Then must I own, I ought not to complain,
Since she nor died, nor did I live in vain.

FINIS.